THE AREA 51 OPTION AND 70 MORE SPECULATIVE FICTION TALES

Michael A. Kechula

BooksForABuck.com
2009

The Area 51 Option and 70 More Speculative Fiction Tales
by Michael A. Kechula

Published by BooksForABuck.com

ISBN: 978-1-60215-107-9

Table of Contents

PUBLICATION HISTORY

$39.50 A PLATE. Alien Skin Magazine 2008.
THE GOLDEN GODDESS. Alien Skin Magazine 2008.
THE SKIM BOX. Word Catalyst Magazine 2007.
FOR WANT OF A DOLLAR. 971 Menu Magazine 2007.
GRAND OPENING. Alien Skin Magazine 2008.
ALL SUGARED UP. From The Asylum Magazine 2007.
HEMINGWAY'S HASHERY. Twisted Tongue Magazine 2008.
PRIMITIVE INSTINCTS. Bewildering Stories 2007.
FUNERAL DAYS. Alien Skin Magazine 2008.
A CHINTZY CARPET. Mirror Dance Magazine 2008.
JUNGLE ROT. Demonic Tome Magazine 2008.
THE PINK CONTRACT. Apollo's Lyre Magazine 2005.
PAYBACK. Ethereal Tales Magazine (England) 2009.
GOOD HOUSE PETS. Short Humour Magazine (England) 2008.
HARD LESSONS OF HISTORY. Muse Marquee Magazine 2008.
A DEEP CUT. Grim Graffiti Magazine 2007.
M. Micro Horror Magazine 2007.
HISTORICAL PERFORMANCE. Ethereal Tales Magazine (England) 2009.
A PREEMPTIVE STRIKE. Big Pulp Magazine 2008.
I SHALL RETURN. Liquid Imagination Magazine 2008.
THE CONTRACT. Short Humour Magazine (England) 2008.
RAZZLE DAZZLE. Dark Wine And Stars Magazine 2009.
GRAND ENTRANCE. Clockwise Cat Magazine 2009.
BLUEBERRY PIE. New Myths Magazine 2008.
FIRST DAY OF SCHOOL. Alien Skin Magazine 2008.
THE CHERRY BOMB. Why Vandalism? Magazine 2007.
RED DUST. Flashes In The Dark Magazine 2009.
THE SPIRITS KNOW ALL. Sonar 4 Magazine 2008.
GOT MILK? Sonar 4 Magazine 2008.
THE ANNIVERSARY PARTY. Alien Skin Magazine 2008.
A WONDERFUL GIFT. Flash Flooding Magazine 2007.
RAH-RAH-SHISH-BOOM-SNAKE. Lotus Blooms Journal 2005. This story won first prize in their writing contest.
UNSPEAKABLE MISERY. Micro Horror Magazine 2007.
FLEA MARKET SPECIAL. Micro Horror Magazine 2007.
A COFFIN IS A WONDROUS THING. Word Slaw Magazine 2008.
ICE CREAM SCOOPS. The Monsters Next Door Magazine. This story won third place in their writing contest.

THE REFUND. Micro Horror Magazine 2007.
A ROUGH CHOICE. The Fiction Flyer Magazine 2008.
SAGE ADVICE. Clockwise Cat Magazine 2008.
TRANSFORMATIONS. Everyday Fiction. 2007.
JAKE'S NEW MEDICINE. Serendipity Magazine (England) 2008.
HIGH FEVER. Colored Chalk 2008.
THE VEIL. Mirror Dance Magazine 2008.
A NATIONAL EMERGENCY. Speculations Magazine 2008.
A BEAUTIFUL DOG EVERY TIME. OMG The Book of Awesome Stuff 2008.
DIGITAL IMAGES. Apollo's Lyre Magazine 2005.
BLESS YOU, DR. PAVLOV. Why Vandalism? Magazine 2008.
PUPPY ISLAND. Clockwise Cat Magazine 2009.
THE AREA 51 OPTION. Mirror Dance Magazine 2009.
CREAMIES. Alien Skin Magazine 2009.
A BIG STOCKHOLDER. Alien Skin Magazine 2009.
THE GREATEST FLAMENCO DANCER IN ALL FLYDOM. Gemini Magazine 2009.
TELL YOU WHAT I'M GONNA DO. Cool Stuff 4 Writers Magazine 2009. This story won first prize in their dialog-only writing contest.
THE WOMAN WITHOUT THE RED DRESS. The New Flesh Magazine 2009.
HIGHWAY 35. The New Flesh Magazine 2009.
NO REPRIEVE. The New Flesh Magazine 2009.
BEFORE AND AFTER. Postcard Shorts Magazine 2009.
DON'T MESS WITH SETI. Postcard Shorts Magazine 2009.
A BIG WAD OF CASH. Postcard Shorts Magazine 2009.
FOOD FADS. Postcard Shorts Magazine 2009.
ZANKER'S SERUM. Postcard Shorts Magazine 2009.
AMNESIA. Postcard Shorts Magazine 2009.
RETALIATION. Postcard Shorts Magazine 2009.
BACK HOME AFTER WAR'S END. Postcard Shorts Magazine 2009.
A VITAL QUESTION. Alien Skin Magazine 2008.
A WONDERFUL BIRD. Alien Skin Magazine 2008.
MARTIAN BEAUTY STANDARDS. Postcard Shorts Magazine 2009.
DIVINE MISSION. Postcard Shorts Magazine 2009.
CHARLIE'S AMAZING BATHING SUIT. Postcard Shorts Magazine 2009.
DISBELIEF. The New Flesh Magazine 2009.
BOREDOM. Flashes In The Dark Magazine 2009.

$39.50 A PLATE

Billions were petrified when Mars was larger than the full Moon in the night sky.

Believers packed houses of worship around the clock. Interpreters of arcane texts warned of Armageddon. Governments tried desperately to reassure the masses. "Yes the Moon will once again become brighter than Mars. No, the Martians aren't going to attack. Yes, Mars will soon return to its usual place in the solar system. No, chickens aren't laying eggs with maroon yolks."

The night Mars was closer than ever, I picked up a blonde female hitchhiker.

"Where you headed?" I asked.

"To the nearest restaurant."

"Next one's 150 miles from here. A fast food joint right before Las Vegas. If you're hungry, I got homemade cookies."

"What's cookies?"

"These are cookies. Chocolate chip cookies."

She put one to her nose. "I don't like the smell. Reminds me of stale Martian spaghetti."

I took the cookie she sniffed and tossed it out the window. Who knows what might've dripped on it? Wiping my hand on my pants, I wished I had some anti-bacterial spray.

"Look, up ahead," she exclaimed. "There's a neon sign. Harry's Desert Diner. Special Today. Martian Spaghetti. $39.50 a Plate. I love Martian spaghetti when it's fresh. I'll bet they just got a shipment."

Nothing was in sight. What a weirdo. Who knows what she might pull. I stopped my rig and ordered her out.

Back at cruising speed, I tuned in a radio talk show. The host described how Planet X would soon strike Mars and Earth.

A caller said it was too bad Mars was gonna be destroyed. He'd never again get a chance to go there and have that delicious, fresh Martian spaghetti. His voice broke with emotion.

When asked what fresh Martian spaghetti tasted like, the caller couldn't describe the experience.

The host asked if anything on Earth was comparable. Maybe something we could get at a supermarket.

"No. But, I can tell you this: stale Martian spaghetti reminds me of Earth's chocolate chip cookies."

Reaching over to grab a country and western CD, I suddenly saw a flashing neon sign.

What the hell? That sign wasn't here when I passed this way two nights ago with a load for the Tropicana Casino.

The sign said, "Harry's Desert Diner. Special Today. Martian Spaghetti. $39.50 a Plate."

Curious, I pulled into the empty parking lot.

Once inside, I nearly fell over when I saw the blonde from my truck sitting at the counter, slurping what looked like red spaghetti.

I took a seat at the counter. A waitress came over, poured coffee, and handed me a menu.

"What's the blonde having?" I asked.

"Today's special. Fresh Martian spaghetti. Want a plate?"

"Not for $39.50."

"We got half-size orders for twenty-five."

"What about a kid's plate."

"You look older than six to me."

"Well, at least tell me how much you charge for a kid's portion."

"Fifteen bucks. Crayons and pictures of famous Martians to color are complimentary. Look, $39.50 is cheap. This is fresh today. Just came in from Area 51. You ain't gonna find better. Not even in Vegas."

"Can I have a sample?"

"No free samples."

"Not even a strand?"

"Nope. Why don't you ask the blonde to share some of hers?"

I went over. "Hi."

"Oh you. The guy with the cookies. Their stench almost ruined my appetite."

"How'd you get here so fast?" I asked.

"Rolled."

"You from Mars?"

"Yeah."

"What brings you here?"

"Mars is doomed. Planet X is gonna ram it. Figured it was worth coming here to stay alive another month."

"Is it really gonna hit Earth after Mars?"

"Yeah, a week after Mars is obliterated."

"Since we're as good as goners, can I have a taste of your Martian spaghetti?"

"Sure, for ten dollars a forkful."

I paid her and rolled some onto a fork. Once inside my mouth, the strands became animated, wiggling under their own power. I spat them out, except for one that wrapped itself around an incisor. Yanking as hard as I could, I was unable to dislodge it.

"Try extra spicy mustard," the blonde said, scooping up the ejected strands from the floor and returning them to her plate.

I squeezed the plastic bottle until my mouth overflowed. The strand emitted a high-pitched squeal, disengaged, and hit the floor.

The blonde picked it up and tossed it down her throat. "Hate to see good food wasted," she said. "Forgot to tell you. You're supposed to toss the strands down your throat. Don't ever let Martian spaghetti linger in your mouth. The sight of teeth scares them, and they can get quite violent. Put yourself in their shoes. What would you do if you saw big white fangs coming at you to crush you from both ends? It's a matter of self defense."

I ran to my truck and fired up the engine.

I was glad Mars would be destroyed, along with all it's stockpiles of spaghetti.

Munching on the remaining chocolate chip cookies, I felt grateful to their benevolent inventors. They had the foresight to devise tasty food that remained passive in the mouth, and didn't mind being masticated for the good of Earthkind. I resolved, should Earth be spared, to build a monument to commemorate chocolate chip cookies and all who were instrumental in their development.

I spent the rest of the trip trying to come up with a suitable epitaph.

THE GOLDEN GODDESS

Weird things began to happen after Sam stole the gold statue of the Smiling Chinese Goddess.

The first night, he stashed the three-inch, ancient statue inside a vase. The next morning he was startled to find the goddess smirking at him from the dining room table. He racked his brain trying to remember when he'd moved it.

Sam left the patio door open when he went to sun himself. He heard something scraping against the concrete patio. Seeing nothing, he went back to his detective novel. Suddenly, a brilliant reflection struck the corner of his glasses. He raced to the edge of the patio. Just in time. The statue looked as if it were about to burrow into the grassy knoll leading to a bamboo garden.

That's when he noticed a strange voice in his head. "Take me back home," the voice said.

At first, he easily dismissed what he thought vivid imagination. But soon, he had to exert considerable effort to silence the intrusive, pleading voice.

The stupid thing's trying to get away. Now it's talking to me. Statues can't talk. This one must be possessed by evil spirits. Maybe I should hire Chinese exorcists to purge them. Damn! What the hell am I saying? I must be going bonkers. I better have a big slug of scotch.

As the days passed, no matter where Sam put the statue, it showed up somewhere else.

"All right, where the hell are you now? I remember stashing you in the center drawer inside my argyle socks."

"You'll never find me," the voice taunted.

"Wrong," Sam said loudly, rooting in the bathroom hamper. "I'm the best burglar in the business. I can find anything."

The moment he saw the lump within a soggy washcloth, Sam yanked the cloth from the hamper, put it on the sink, and untied it. "How the hell did you manage to tie this thing on the outside when you're on the inside?" he yelled at the sneering statue.

"I want to go back home," the voice insisted for the hundredth time.

"When Danson arrives from London for the swap, you'll have a fine new home, in wonderful surroundings. Not like the dinky hole-in-the wall you had before. And I'll have a fine new home too. A mansion in Mexico, thanks to you." Sam chuckled with pleasure when he thought of the three million Danson offered for the ancient, solid gold artifact.

"I don't want a new home." The voice whined from somewhere deep within Sam's skull.

Sam dropped the frowning statue into a glass jar. Tightening the lid with all his might, he shoved the jar into the microwave. For a moment, he wished the statue were organic so he could fry the damn thing.

He couldn't wait until he could fence the statue. It'd been nothing but a headache. But, Danson said he'd need two weeks to raise the cash. Sam began to wonder if he could last until Danson's arrival.

Two days before Danson was due, a tattoo suddenly appeared on the back of Sam's left hand. Petrified, he soiled his underwear.

When regaining his composure, he examined the tattoo's oriental pictograph. "What the hell does this mean?" he shouted at the glowering statue inside the microwave.

Racing to a Chinese restaurant, Sam asked the middle-aged owner to translate the tattoo.

"You don't know what you had tattooed on your own hand?"

"I was drunk. I told the guy to do whatever he wanted."

"It looks Chinese. But I don't know what it says. Maybe my uncle knows."

The old man looked through spectacles with lenses thick as the bottoms of shot glasses. "It say, 'whoever...read...tattoo...must...immediately.'"

"Must immediately what?"

"It not say."

Sam thanked the man and left. Back home, he cursed the statue, now baring its teeth. "I don't care what the hell you try to pull. In three days you're outta here, and I'm in three million."

The next morning, Sam found a new tattoo. This time on the back of his right hand. After downing three double scotches in rapid succession, he hurried to the Chinese restaurant.

"Can I see your uncle again?"

The uncle adjusted his glasses and stared at the new tattoo. He shouted something in Chinese, then collapsed.

Within seconds, the restaurant filled with panicked relatives. An old woman grabbed Sam's hands and read aloud, "Whoever reads these tattoos must immediately kill the wearer or die in his place."

"I cannot kill," she said, grabbing her chest and falling to the floor.

All shielded their eyes, as Sam ran out.

"Stop him! Murderer! Don't look at his tattoos."

Sam ran for his life. Turning a corner, he slammed into a cop.

"Hey! What the hell's going on?"

"I didn't do anything, Officer. An old guy and woman looked at my tattoos to translate them. They both fell over. Just like that. I didn't touch them. I swear."

"Let me see the tattoos. Hmm. This is very old Chinese. Sonovabitch!"

The cop pulled his pistol and fired point blank into Sam's face.

A sweet, serene smile replaced the golden goddess's homicidal sneer.

THE SKIM BOX

"Quick! I need change for the phone. There's a woman lying on the pavement. She may be dead."

The fry cook flashed a frosty, get-lost look at Mike, then resumed his late night conversation with a customer.

"If you don't believe me, look for yourself." Mike hoped the dare added authenticity to his plea. All he needed was a lousy dime to call the cops.

Acting as if he'd been asked to donate blood to save the guy who raped his sister, the cook yanked the dollar bill from Mike's hand, slammed the no sale key, and slapped coins into Mike's palm.

Mike ran to the wall phone, inserted a dime, and dialed 0. "I tripped over a woman's body," he told the operator, who immediately rang the police.

The phone rang at least a dozen times. *Where are the cops?*

He glanced out the window, just as a foot patrolman walked by. Hanging up, he grabbed the refunded dime, and ran outside.

The cop had moved the woman into a doorway. Her head flopped back and forth, as he shook her shoulders. "Wake up, Martha," he said loudly. "How many times have I told you to stay off my beat when you're drunk?"

When he shook her again, she responded by hurling vomit onto his uniform. "Sonovabitch!" he yelled, making a hasty exit. Martha's legs gave way, and she slid back onto the pavement.

Mike leaned close to her face. The stench of vomit and alcohol turned his stomach. "Are you OK?" he asked.

Martha's eyes popped open. "Damn cop! Leave me alone!" Throwing her hands to his face, she dug fingernails into his cheeks.

He recoiled from the sharp sting of her vicious attack. Running down the street, he pressed a handkerchief to his face. A street light showed dark blotches smeared across white cotton.

His watch showed 1:40 AM. Playing Good Samaritan made him miss the last bus from Manhattan to New Jersey, by ten minutes. Now, he'd have to wait four hours. There was no place to go—everything was closed. He couldn't even wait inside the bus terminal—they'd never installed benches.

Mike thought of the bus departure area on the fourth floor. It was like an outdoor parking garage. If he went there, at least he could sit on the ground.

As expected, the departure area was a morgue—cold, silent, isolated. He tried to read a paperback, but the overhead lights were too dim. He tried to doze, but couldn't get comfortable on the frozen concrete. Shivering, he thought about the Martha fiasco. *Why didn't I just keep walking when I tripped over Martha's body? I'd be home and under the covers by now.*

At the peak of frustration, the terminal door flew open. A man stepped through, singing loudly, "Eh-Mambo...Mambo Italiano...Eh-Mambo...Mambo Italiano...."

Mike hadn't heard that bouncy Rosemary Clooney tune in ages. Ten years before, in the early '50s it'd been the favorite song of his best buddy, Tony Coco—Coconuts.

Long forgotten feelings of sadness and missing Coconuts, struck him with surprising intensity.

The well-dressed stranger sang louder as he mambo'd toward Mike. His arms were extended as if holding an imaginary partner. "Eh-Mambo...Mambo Italiano...Eh-Mambo...Mambo Italiano...." he sang, gliding forward and sideways. "Go, go, go you mixed up Siciliano...All you Calabrese do the mambo like-a crazy...."

Mike was glad to see another human being, but wondered how anybody could be so exuberant at 2:15 AM, especially on such a cold night.

Suddenly, the man stopped singing. "Hey Mikey," he called. "How you doing, old buddy?"

Mike didn't recognize the stranger.

"Don't you recognize me all grown up?"

"Coconuts?" Mike stood, fighting an impulse to run to the stranger and throw arms around him.

"None other. At your service, Mikey Kay."

Only Coconuts had ever called Michael Antonio Kaczmarczyk by that name.

"But Coconuts is—"

"It's a matter of belief," the stranger said, extending his hand.

Mike didn't lift his hand, but the stranger grabbed and shook it vigorously. Contrary to expectations, the stranger's hand was warm. This was bewildering. If he weren't so exhausted, Mike would have run for the nearest exit.

"I don't understand. I was at your—uh—Tony Coco's fun—"

"It was a nice one too. Right after my thirteenth birthday. Remember the thirteen flower cars that Snuffy sent?" The stranger chuckled. "He musta bought up all the flowers from Paterson to Newark. Remember why?"

Mike's mouth went dry; his hands trembled.

"You look scared, Mikey Kay. Relax. The Capo Di Capo sent me." He pointed upward. "You know—the Boss of Bosses. Hey, you'll be glad I came. Now, tell me why Snuffy bought up all the flowers in North Jersey?"

"Because—" Mike's teeth chattered so much he couldn't form the words.

"Because why? C'mon—you know the answer," the stranger said playfully. "Don't be afraid to say it."

"Because he accidentally shot—"

"Bata-bing!" That's how Coconuts had always confirmed a correct answer. "Bang, bang, bang!" The stranger said, his hand imitating a pistol.

Mike couldn't stop shaking. He thought about making a run for the door. He tried to remember the prayer his Italian grandma had taught him to dispel evil apparitions.

"Take it easy, Mikey. I won't hurt you. I just wanted to hear somebody say what happened. I've been away so long. So many have forgotten. Think hard. What happened when Snuffy shot up my dad's store?"

"A bullet ricocheted."

"Bata-bing! I was in the back eating cannoli. Then, wham! My last bite of food for eternity. You know, Mikey, I really miss cannoli. Will you eat one for me, tomorrow?"

"Sh—Sure."

"The connoli at Rocco's on Passaic Street is the best. Where they hang the salamis and provolones from the ceiling. It'll be fun watching half-a-Wop eating cannoli. What's your other half? I forget."

"Ukrainian."

"Never could spell your Uky name," the stranger said. "How about spelling it for me, one more time, Mikey?"

"K-A-C-Z-M-A-R-C-Z-Y-K."

"Those C's and Z's always mixed me up. Me, who always got A's on my spelling tests at Number 12 School. Hey—I guess you're wondering why I'm here."

Mike nodded slightly, knees knocking.

"Can you believe they made me a Rewarding Angel? I check the books of good deeds, to make sure people are rewarded. Every unselfish deed is recorded in the books. I looked up your name. Your accounts are out of balance."

"Out of balance?"

"Yep. I'm here to fix that. You're overdue to receive your just deserts."

"My just deserts?" Mike felt a tinge of relief.

"I brought you something special—a map to Snuffy's skim box. He used it to stash all the money he skimmed from numbers collections. A little at a time, so nobody'd notice. Over the years, he stashed fifty thousand. He died yesterday. Shoot-out in Newark. Nobody knows about the skim box he buried by the river. Now it's yours." He passed the map to Mike.

Mike stared at the map with unbelieving eyes.

"Mikey, don't let a bunch of thankless fools, like Martha, change you. Keep on filling up pages in the good books. Rewards may be delayed, but I guarantee they'll show up. Charity and compassion are always rewarded."

He turned away, began dancing the mambo, and headed for the terminal door. "Eh-Mambo...Mambo Italiano...Eh-Mambo..."

The door opened on it's own. The stranger disappeared inside the terminal.

Fifty thousand dollars! More than I can earn in ten years!

His mind flooded with visions of lollygagging at Miami Beach; hanging around Hollywood to glimpse Marilyn Monroe, Sandra Dee, Lucille Ball; playing golf with Bob Hope and Bing Crosby.

He laughed hysterically. Suddenly, he raced for the door to the terminal.

"Coconuts!" he yelled, yanking the door open.

He looked around and saw nothing but sterile marble walls. He brought both hands to his mouth forming a megaphone. "I promise I'll get a cannoli, tomorrow. I hate that stuff. But, I'll go to Rocco's and eat one anyway. Just for you."

His words bounced off empty terminal walls.

FOR WANT OF A DOLLAR

Talbot saw an intriguing ad in the morning paper: "Relive the Past. Not Yours. Somebody Else's. Call for Details."

Disgusted with his miserable life, Talbot dialed the number.

"Past Lives Incorporated. Zero speaking."

"I'm calling about your ad. What does it cost to relive somebody else's past?"

"Ten thousand dollars."

"Aw, hell. I shoulda known you guys were fast-buck artists."

"I assure you, Sir, we're a highly respected, legitimate corporation. In fact we're listed on the New York Stock Exchange. We're registered with the Better Business Bureau, and we sponsor a Little League team. Plus we have plenty of references from highly satisfied customers. Many are very famous people whose names you'd recognize immediately. Right now we're having an end-of-month sale."

"Sale or no, I can't afford thousands of dollars."

"Perhaps we can work something out. This is our slowest time of year. How about a dollar...and your soul? You'll have the time of your life. Guaranteed, or double your money back."

Thirty minutes later, Talbot was in the Past Lives office.

"Whose past would you like to relive?" Zero asked.

"Julius Caesar's."

"Wonderful choice! Checking a computer printout, Zero added, "Right now Caesar's last twenty years are available. Do you mind at the end of twenty years being dispatched by multiple stab wounds at the hands of Brutus and his gang? For an additional dollar, we can arrange to make it painless."

"What happens after he stabs me?"

"You'll die, of course. But when you're dead, we can bring you back to life for another dollar. Guaranteed. How can you lose? Wanna make a deal to relive Caesar's last twenty years?"

"Yeah."

"Good. That'll be a dollar, plus another dollar to make your stabbing painless. As to your soul, we won't require that today. Our soul extractors are booked solid for the next year."

Talbot paid and signed the contract.

"When do you wanna get started?" Zero asked.

"How about tonight?"

"Sure. Take this pill before bedtime. It'll put you into a deep sleep so we can transfer your brain waves and vital essences. When you wake up, you'll be in Julius Caesar's body. By the way, you'll be in Gallia Transalpina."

"Where's that?"

"It's the old name for the area around France and Switzerland. It's gonna be chilly."

"Should I wear a coat to bed?"

"No. You'll wake up wearing Caesar's winter clothes. By the way, you're scheduled to lead Roman legions in battle tomorrow at sunrise. In case you're not familiar with Roman history, you're gonna whip the hell out Vercingetorix."

"Who's he?"

"A two-bit, renegade, tribal Chief. The idiot drank too much wine and threatened Rome. Caesar's gonna teach him a lesson. Actually, it'll be over in a few hours, with you the winner. Included in the spoils will be his magnificent daughter. She'll be your slave for the next ten years. Think you can handle an eighteen year old, wanton wildcat tomorrow night?"

Talbot had a fabulous time whipping Vercingetorix and his tribesmen. His night with Vercingetorix's insatiable daughter was indescribable.

Reliving Caesar's past was more fun than Talbot had imagined. Especially since Caesar's last twenty years had been filled with wine, women, and song, with some wars tossed in for diversion.

For nineteen years and eleven months, Talbot Caesar had the time of his life. As the days dwindled, he recalled his high school history lesson about Brutus's dirty deed. Brutus was due to assassinate Caesar in two weeks. Talbot decided to beat him to the punch with a preemptive strike. He figured if he eliminated his assassin, he could extend Caesar's life long enough to be declared Emperor.

"Imagine," Talbot muttered. "I only paid a buck to end up as the next Emperor of the entire Roman Empire. What a helluva deal!"

Eleven days before zero hour, Brutus jumped Caesar and stabbed him as he approached the Forum. Stunned, Talbot Caesar said, "What the hell are you doing? You're way off schedule."

"Nay," Brutus replied, plunging a knife into Caesar's heart. "Today is the Ides of March."

As he drew his last breath, Talbot heard somebody calling his name.

"Hey, Talbot. Welcome to Gehenna."

"What the hell am I doing here?" he asked Zero.

"You ain't here. Your soul is. Remember our deal?"

"Yeah. Damn it's hot. Stinks too. Who are all those ugly broads?"

"Your tormentors."

"Hey, that wasn't in the contract."

"Wrong. It was in the small print. Well, you got your twenty years as promised. Now, I have your soul. Did I ever tell you how I loathe mankind? And that I'm a hyper-sadist?"

"This can't be. I was all set to wipe out Brutus in a preemptive strike. But he got me first. I can't figure how."

"Maybe somebody tipped him off," Zero said with a fiendish grin. "Well, no matter. You're mine now."

"Wait! You said for a dollar I could be brought back to life."

"True. Got one?"

"Sure." Talbot reaching into his toga and removed some Roman coins.

"Our deal was for a US dollar, not some worthless Roman coins," Zero said.

"Would somebody please lend me a dollar?" Talbot yelled to the horrid entities moving toward him.

Before he could ask again, tormentors pulled him into a flaming pit.

GRAND OPENING

When Bert graduated from Acme Mortician School, he startled the funeral home community by opening the first drive-thru funeral business in America. To ensure everybody was aware of his innovation, he bombarded the public with radio, TV, and newspaper ads.

"Fed up with costly funerals? Bring your loved ones to Bert's Drive-Thru Cut-Rate Funeral Emporium where funerals are only $39.95. How can we offer such bargain basement prices? We use machines instead of morticians. All you have to do is put the deceased in your car, and drop him off at our super-convenient, self-service Drive-Thru. And while you're here, stay for the show. Watch on giant, outdoor, high definition TVs how corpses are processed in our fully automated Funeral Emporium. New show starts every thirty minutes. And don't forget to come to our grand opening celebration on Labor Day. The first fifty customers who bring a corpse will enjoy a free buffet lunch at our new restaurant, The Happy Cadaver. Save mega-bucks on your next funeral. Bring your loved ones to Bert's Drive-Thru Cut-Rate Funeral Emporium."

The commercials always ended with Bert singing, "There's no business like show business."

Bert's advertising campaign worked. Hundreds of cars, trucks, vans, station wagons, SUVS, motor homes, and tour busses showed up on opening day. However, two hours after the ribbon cutting ceremony, not a single corpse had been dropped off at the Drive-Thru. Bert had to cancel the first four shows.

Visitors became restless. Many honked, hooted, whistled, booed, cursed.

Harry, the funeral home's only employee, spoke to the crowd through the public address system.

"Ladies and Gentlemen, we're sorry for the delay. Frankly, we hoped some of you would have brought a deceased body or two. So, what we'd like you to do right now is to check everyone in your vehicles to see if any of them might be on the verge of dying. The first person who brings a fresh corpse to our Drive-Thru in the next five minutes will get a special bonus."

"What's the bonus?" somebody yelled from an SUV.

"A hundred dollars. Plus a free buffet lunch at our new restaurant, The Happy Cadaver.

When nobody came forth, Harry said, "Are you sure there aren't any seniors out there who are on the verge of heart failure? How about potential massive strokes? Any aneurisms about to burst?"

Still no response.

"What about suicides? Anybody here fed up with life? Anybody with nerves frazzled so bad, they can't go on? How about deep depression? Anybody in utter despair? If so, come forward, and we'll be happy to help. We have a fine selection of cyanide pills, ropes, razor blades—just about anything you need to end it all."

"We got a dead body over here!" somebody yelled from a battered Toyota. "Granny just slipped and banged her head against a door handle. She ain't got no pulse. And she's bleedin' all over the place."

Nobody knew the Toyota's passengers had decided a hundred dollars was far better than having a ninety-year old, sickly grandma hanging around. One of them whacked her head with a tire iron. The driver pulled her bloody body out of the car and dragged it toward Harry.

"Looks like we have a winner," Harry said. "What's the deceased's name?"

"Granny Smith."

"Ladies and gentlemen. I'm pleased to announce we have our very first customer. Let's hear it for Granny Smith."

Visitors applauded, whistled, honked.

Harry helped the bereaved carry the bloody corpse to the Drive-Thru where they dropped her on a gurney. After wiping blood from his hands, Harry called Bert to tell him the good news. Elated, Bert hurried from his office to the Drive-Thru. When he checked the woman, he discovered a faint heartbeat. Disgusted, he called an ambulance.

"False alarm," Harry told disappointed visitors. "Sorry about that. Looks like we still need a corpse."

Some in the crowd booed and threw empty beer bottles at Harry and Bert.

Bert took out his cell phone and acted as if he'd just received a call. Grabbing the microphone, he said, "Ladies and gentlemen, I have good news. I just got word that a body's on the way. The show will start in twenty minutes. In the meantime, visit our snack stands and get a free bag of popcorn."

When applause broke out, he told Harry, "We have a potentially explosive situation here. Let's go to my office where it'll be safer."

On the way, Harry asked Bert why he lied.

"I had to tell them something. They're in a nasty mood. I hope they don't start a riot."

"Maybe we oughta call 911 and ask for a SWAT team."

"I've been thinking the same thing," Bert said. "Especially since it might be a while before a body turns up. Would you believe nobody died over the past two days?"

"How do you know?"

"I called the morgue. Their slabs and refrigerators are empty. Then I called the ambulance service, hoping they had a hit and run victim, or maybe a DUI who might've slammed into a pole. But they had nothing. This is unbelievable for a holiday weekend. I even called my competitors to see if I could borrow a body. But they don't have any. Like me, they can't figure out why there's a sudden dry spell. Maybe it has something to do with global warming."

As they reached the office, Harry asked, "So what are we gonna do?"

"I'm going to ask you to honor the employment agreement you signed."

"Do you mean the clause that said I was subject to lay off if things got tough?"

When Harry fell to the floor with a bullet in his brain, Bert said. "Not that clause. I meant the one where you agreed to do whatever's necessary to meet the needs of the business."

Heading for the Drive-Thru with Harry's body aboard a gurney, Bert sang, "There's no business like show business."

ALL SUGARED UP

"Block the door!" yelled a security guard. "Don't let it escape!"

Three guards jumped in front of the mall exit door.

The naked thing lowered its head and slammed them like a battering ram. The impact was so tremendous, the guards died instantly. The steel exit door behind them flew into the parking garage.

A SWAT team fired automatic weapons at the thing. Unfazed, it rushed toward them. Grabbing the nearest cop, it hurled him a hundred feet. When a burst of machine gun fire blew the thing's neck to smithereens, its head fell off. The headless body lurched forward several feet, then fell to the ground.

"Hold your fire," a police captain yelled. "It's dead."

"It was never alive," said a sergeant, as he walked toward the thing.

"It had to be. Look at the freakin' damage. It knocked that steel door off its hinges like it was made of paper."

"What's that bubbly blue stuff coming from its neck?" somebody asked.

"Look's like some kind of foam," the captain said. "Hey, Charlie, collect some of it in test tubes. Homeland Security would be very interested in this. And probably the FBI, CIA and National Institute of Health."

Some curious shoppers came through the doorway.

"Get those people back in the mall. Seal the place. Get them to announce nobody leaves the mall."

"Hey, something's inside its mouth," yelled a cop checking the severed head.

"What is it?"

"Looks like a bunch of half-chewed jelly beans. Maybe it got all sugared-up and went nuts."

"Unless they really ain't jelly beans," said the captain. "Sergeant, have somebody check the candy store. See if this thing stole some jelly beans."

"I don't get it," the sergeant said. "Since when does a mannequin come to life, steal candy, and go berserk?"

"Weird stuff happens," the lieutenant said. "Like when it rains frogs. Or when they find a whale dying in the middle of the Sahara Desert. In the end, there's always a logical explanation."

"Don't let the press know it was a dummy," the captain said. "Tell them a nude guy went berserk after taking a designer drug. If this ever gets out, wackos will firebomb malls all over the country. They'll buy jelly beans and run through malls yelling, 'I'm a crazed mannequin.'"

"Hey, Harris and Smith," the lieutenant said. "Check out all the mannequins in the mall."

"What do you want us to look for?" Smith asked.

"See if any of them have been chewing jelly beans."

"You gotta be kidding, Lieutenant."

"I wish I was. But the way things are any more, you gotta check every little thing to make damn sure. This could be a terrorist plot."

"What should I do if I find one with jelly beans in its mouth?"

"Arrest the damn thing. Don't forget to read its rights. I don't want some civil rights lawyer getting a mannequin released over a stupid technicality."

Seventy-six mannequins in the mall's department stores had jellybeans in their mouths. Some had wads consisting of several flavors. Others were found chewing only a single flavor. Nobody knew what to make of it.

The FBI went into action and checked every mannequin in the nation. 100,000 were found chewing jellybeans. All were jailed and interrogated. The FBI's worst suspicions were confirmed: this was a terrorist plot of monstrous proportions. The Terrorist Alert was raised two notches around the globe.

Information about potential mannequin attacks was rushed to intelligence agencies of friendly nations. Meanwhile, the 100,000 jailed mannequin prisoners were crated and loaded onto merchant ships. A hundred pounds of jelly beans were included within each crate. The crates were marked: A GIFT FROM THE PEOPLE OF THE UNITED STATES.

* * * *

Countries hostile to the United States marveled at the generosity of Americans when they received shiploads of jelly beans and mannequins they'd never ordered.

HEMINGWAY'S HASHERY

"Hey there," called an armed guard. "You lost?"

"Not exactly," said Bret Harding. "According to my historical research, this is where the town of Stepford once stood."

"Never heard of it," said the guard.

"That was the creepy town where guys turned their wives into robots, making them ravishing creatures of pleasure. Where all the women made endless batches of chocolate chip cookies. The government discovered what was going on, destroyed the town, and jailed all the men. It happened about thirty years ago."

"Doesn't ring a bell," the guard said.

"What's the name of this place?"

"Scriptopia."

"Hmmm. It's not on my Connecticut road map," Harding said.

"This town's very exclusive. Has special status. They kept it off maps and the Global Positioning System. Everything behind this wall ain't part of Connecticut. Just like Washington, D. C. ain't part of Maryland."

"No wonder it isn't on my map. Is this some kind of hush-hush research center like Area 51?"

"Not that I know of. All our residents are writers."

"What kind of writers?"

"Fiction."

"Sounds interesting. How are my chances of getting inside? I'm Bret Harding, instructor of Modern History at Santa Buffoona College, in California. Here's my ID."

After scrutinizing Harding's ID, the guard said, "We usually discourage visitors. But, since you're a college teacher maybe the Sheriff will let you in."

The guard mumbled into a cell phone.

"The Sheriff wants to know if you've ever written a best seller."

"Not yet, but I'm working on it."

"Sheriff Spitz says you can enter under certain conditions. Please raise your right hand. Are you now, or have you ever been a writer of poetry, limericks, greeting card jingles, nursery rhymes, or song lyrics?"

"No," Bret lied, figuring they'd never heard of his three books of esoteric, cryptic, noxious poetry.

"I'm obligated to warn you: poets are strictly forbidden in Scriptopia. Violation of town ordinances carries extremely stiff penalties."

"I understand. Can you point me to a coffee shop? I could use a good cup of brew after driving so long."

"Sure. This is Dostoyevsky Drive. Take this for about a mile, then turn left at Steinbeck Street. It's on the corner. Hemingway's Hashery. Oh, the Sheriff said you can stay for only one hour. Better set a timer. He's one mean SOB. By the way, he writes sock-o detective novels."

Bret almost blurted, "Me too," a fib of monstrous proportions. He couldn't write a piece of readable prose if his life depended on it. But when it came to iambic pentameter, he was a master.

The gates swung open.

Bret drove down a tree-lined avenue. "Get a load of that," he mumbled when he saw lampposts shaped like fountain pens.

Beautiful brick homes came into view. The chimneys of some emitted puffs of gray smoke. He had to glance twice when a smoke cloud suddenly formed a bubble in which appeared the words, "IT WAS A DARK AND STORMY NIGHT." Pulling over to the curb, Bret rubbed his eyes in disbelief. *How are they doing that?*

When he looked again, the smoke was gone. But suddenly a second smoke cloud rose from a different house. It formed into, "BRET DROPPED HIS HOT HAND ON CHELSEA'S QUIVERING THIGH." Still another said, "THE ZOMBIE'S EYES GLOWED AS HIS POWERFUL FINGERS GRIPPED MISS POTTER'S CREAMY NECK."

"Holy smoke!" Bret yelled, chills running down his spine. He couldn't wait to get inside the restaurant for a sanity check.

The restaurant, shaped like a giant, old-time, manual typewriter, came into view. Once inside, he noticed the place was as quiet as an Arctic graveyard. Everywhere he looked, customers were eating with one hand and scribbling in notebooks with the other. Even the kids.

"Mommy. What do you think of this sentence?" a boy asked quietly. "The werewolf grabbed the vampire and twisted his head off."

"Very nice," said a blonde woman, patting the boy's head. "I think you should add some dialogue. Tell us what the werewolf said. And maybe you can include what the vampire was thinking as his head was being twisted." Then she quickly added, "Better finish your Fiction Fries before they get cold and soggy."

Bret chose a counter seat a few feet from the waitress who was writing furiously in a notebook. Glancing at Bret, she whispered, "I'll be with you soon as I finish this paragraph."

After several minutes of boring silence, he absent-mindedly tapped keys on the counter. Immediately, he was bombarded with shushing sounds and hostile stares. "Sorry," he mumbled.

"Finished," the waitress whispered, glancing at Bret. "Sorry to make you wait. Didn't wanna break my thoughts. Been struggling over that paragraph all morning."

Her happy-face nametag announced, "Becky Bunky. Author of The Moiling Mob. 10 weeks on the NY Times Best Seller List."

"Wow," he whispered. "I see, Becky Bunky, thee art she who wrote a bigee."

"What did you say?" the woman asked sharply.

Oh, hell! I goofed. "I said that I see you've hit the big time, with your book being a best seller."

"No you didn't. I distinctly heard you say something that sounded like a poem. You a poet?" she yelled loudly.

"No. I'm a history teacher."

Suddenly, customers surrounded Bret. "You a poet?" they chanted in unison, repeating it a dozen times.

The Sheriff stormed in. Handcuffing Bret, he yelled, "You were warned at the gate, Harding. We don't want any damn poets around here. We're all refugees from that abominable trash that uses countless, meaningless, mind-bending words to say nothing. It's five years since somebody tried to sneak in here and convert us from prose writers to poetry hacks. Do you realize what you've done? Look at all the kids here munching on Homonym Hamburgers, Simile Sausages, and Personification Pancakes. You've contaminated their malleable minds. Do you think we want them running around yelling, "Rosy-posy-chewy-dewy-hokey-smoky?" It's downright pornographic, you sleazy malefactor!"

Searching Bret, the Sheriff pulled a petite volume of sonnets from his coat pocket. "Here's proof!" yelled the Sheriff, holding the book high for all to see.

Women shrieked, men blanched, oldsters threw up, parents shielded children's eyes to prevent trauma.

That night, the townsfolk gathered to watch Bret Harding walk barefoot across ten feet of white-hot train rails. Wearing a dunce cap, on which was written, "POET," Bret never got past the first few inches. When his feet burst into flames, he toppled headfirst into a pit of blazing embers.

"Look," somebody yelled, as a cloud of smoke rose from Bret's charred corpse. Inside the cloud appeared the words, "A POX ON THEE FOR KILLING ME."

"What does that say, Mommy?"

"Nothing. It's just a stupid poem."

"What's a poem?"

"The ravings of demons," she snapped. "You better forget you ever heard that terrible word. If I ever hear you saying it, I'll wash your mouth out with soap and sell you to the Gypsies."

PRIMITIVE INSTINCTS

The grassy knoll was damp on Christmas Eve when Harry peered through his night scope, selected a target, then fired.

The target's head exploded.

"One shot, one kill," he muttered as he scooted back down the hole, slid the grassy lid over the top, and threw the locking latches. Then he ran like hell through the polymer tunnels of the Doomsday Shelter, the complex he'd designed back in 2075. Back when the US government expended 22 trillion to construct a global network of interconnecting, subterranean shelters designed to save the population in case of all-out alien attack.

Reaching the rocket sled, he pressed the ignition. As he sped at mach 8 through the tubes from the hills of Virginia to his base in Australia, he waited for the inevitable 3.5 Richter scale quake the Martians generated to retaliate after each night's kill.

The bastards were smart enough to take over the Earth and liquidate its entire population in three days. But they're incredible idiots when it comes to geology. I designed this complex to withstand 15.5 on the Richter scale. One day they'll find out, but by then, I'll be long dead. I still can't believe I'm the last human on the planet. Damn good thing I was inspecting the underground storage terminals twenty miles below the Great Barrier Reef when they struck. Otherwise, I would've been vaporized along with the rest.

Bowing his head, he observed a moment of silence for the masses that'd died during the Martian siege.

Arriving at his base under the former city of Sydney, Australia, he drew another line on the kill chart. An automated voice reminded him this was kill number 1,083.

He had found enough ammunition to kill another 100,000 of the bastards. If he continued to assassinate them at one per night, he figured it'd take a little over 273 years to reach that number. On the other hand, if he upped the nightly kill to ten, he could take out that many in twenty-seven years. His New Year's resolution was to increase his nightly kills to ten.

With a bottle of whiskey in one hand, and a candy cane in the other, he flopped on a sofa and sang Jingle Bells. He sipped the bottle until he passed out.

On Christmas morning, as he'd done every year since the Martians imposed the final solution, he checked under the faux fireplace.

"Thank you," Santa he said, reaching for the dozens of gifts he'd wrapped for himself. "Next year, I hope you drop a female down the chimney."

Grabbing enough ration packets to have a luscious Christmas dinner, he rode his rocket sled to Tuvalu, a Pacific island not yet occupied by Martian hordes.

When he exited the camouflaged polymer tube on Tuvalu's white sandy beach, he spotted a coconut. It'd make a wonderful desert. Though he had a stash of well over a billion rich, packaged deserts from every nation, there was nothing like eating something fresh. Especially when lying on a fabulous, sun-drenched beach cooled by gentle, Pacific breezes.

Staring up into the sky, he thought he saw something heading in the direction of Tuvalu.

Must be one of those Martian's supply ships. Their settlement teams are probably getting closer to Tuvalu. I'll have to find another place to come out for fresh air.

Then he noticed the flying object didn't have the silhouette of a Martian freighter. He hoped it came from Venus, or Saturn, and that it carried an invasion force to wipe out the Martians. Anything would be better than those genocidal bastards.

Suddenly, the object turned and headed toward him. Grabbing his rifle, he raced for the exit. Before he could reach it, something struck his back and knocked him to the ground.

"What the hell is this?" he hollered, picking up the thing that'd downed him. "Geez! A real snowball?"

Another one whizzed past his ear. He raised his rifle, but it fell from his hands when he saw reindeer pulling a sleigh.

"Harry, you son-of-a-gun. I've been looking all over for you. I've been trying to deliver something to you for the past three Christmases."

Santa pointed to a block of ice in the back of his sleigh. "Well, don't just stand there. Push it into your shelter. It'll defrost in twelve hours. Here's the instructions. Hurry! Those lousy Martians are liable to lock onto my sleigh any second. I don't know when I can make it back, again. Merry Christmas."

Santa jumped into his sleigh, and was gone in a flash.

Harry snapped out of his stupor and pushed the block of ice to the entrance tube.

When he returned home, he read the instructions.

"Inside the block of ice is a female creature from another galaxy. It's the best I could do under the circumstances. She's about two-hundred Earth years old, but has the mind of a child. She has powerful, primitive instincts, including the one you want most. Speak into any of the ten openings on her head, and she'll understand. She has a built-in language translator."

Harry couldn't wait to defrost her.

When she awoke, her four arms reached out. Gently pulling her to him, he spread her feathers and whispered a question into one of her head openings. She nodded. Taking his hand, she pressed it against each of the seven apertures that ran along her outermost tentacle.

"Mmm. One for every day of the week," he said, kissing her first set of lips, then the pair just above.

She quivered.

"That's lesson number one," he said, gazing deeply into the orange eye in the middle of her scaled forehead. "Before we move on to lesson two—do you mind if I call you Eve?"

He thought he heard the most charming, girlish giggle.

FUNERAL DAYS

"Bingo-dingo!" Bert exclaimed when he finally saw restaurant icons on Interstate 80, somewhere in the boonies of Wyoming. "I'm so damn hungry, I could eat a whole cow."

Taking the next exit, he drove the two miles to the small town of Wghaf.

Driving through the center of town, he noticed black bunting on all lampposts. A black banner stretching across the street announced, "Funeral Days July 20 - 31."

What a wacky sense of humor these folks have. They must be having one helluva wild rodeo. Funeral days. I guess they mean killer bulls and bone-busting broncos.

Going into a restaurant, he sat at the counter.

"Welcome to Wghaf," said a cute waitress, who made the name sound like "wig-half."

"Is that an Indian name?"

"Nope," she said, handing him a menu.

"In Arizona," he said, "there's a town called, Bucket of Blood. Named by some cowboys after a big shootout."

"Wghaf ain't no cowboy name. Did you ever hear of a cowboy named Wghaf?"

"Can't say that I have."

"Well, if you must know, it's one of them acro-nims. Stands for We're Gonna Have A Funeral."

"Ah, I get it. Wghaf and Funeral Days. Nice tie-in. So what's going on, a big rodeo?"

"Nope. Funeral Days is when we celebrate all the live births of the past year."

Bert figured he was right about the town folk having one helluva weird sense of humor. "Next you'll tell me they throw a big blast for all the still born and miscarriages."

"Yep. Day after Halloween. Now, that's the time to be in town. There's fantastic parties. Would-have-been dads pass out cigars. We put up a gigantic birthday cake in the middle of Main Street. It says, "Happy Birthday, Nobody." Everybody lines up and throws rocks at it. Afterward, we all take turns sliding through the icing. It's a great time. Maybe you saw pictures about it in Wyoming Backroads magazine."

"Different strokes for different folks," Bert said, sickened at the thought of such a loony celebration. Why go to outer space when we got so much weird right on this planet?

"So, what'll you have?" she asked.

"Chili with lotsa cheddar and onions. Corn bread with honey butter."

She scribbled on a pad and headed for the kitchen.

A few minutes later she served his lunch.

"Bingo-dingo," Bert said when shoveling in a spoonful of chili. "This is the best I've had in ages."

"What'd you say?" asked the waitress with a stunned look.

"Bingo-dingo. Why?"

A hush fell over the room. Suddenly everyone was on their knees, hands raised to heaven, shouting, "Bingo-dingo...bingo-dingo...bingo-dingo."

The sound carried outside. Cars stopped. Passengers got out and fell to their knees, yelling, "Bingo-dingo."

People poured out of mom-and-pop shops. All fell to their knees, joyfully crying out, "Bingo-dingo."

Soon, the entire town was on its knees, hands raised high, faces glowing ecstatically, yelling the same word repeatedly, until everyone collapsed.

Then, all was deathly quiet.

Bert was so shocked, he headed for his car to get the hell out of there. Problem was, too many bodies blocked his way. He started to pull people away from the car so he could back out.

Some came to. Then others. They began to surround Bert. A beautiful woman approached with awe and called him, "Holy Father."

A man touched him, bowed, and said, "Eternal Redeemer."

Before long, he was surrounded by hundreds of adoring Wghafonians.

The Sheriff approached. "Welcome, Master, Oh Great Seer of the Universe."

Raising him to shoulder height, they carried Bert like a renowned football hero to the finest hotel room in town.

"Bingo-dingo," the Mayor said, "is the sacred word we've been waited to hear for countless generations. The Holy Scroll says, "He will come on the last day of the festival and say to one and all, "Bingo-dingo." And now you've come. We are ready to immolate ourselves as the Scroll directs, to gain our eternal reward and free the souls of our ancestors."

Bert couldn't dissuade the Mayor. After all, he was dealing with a deeply engrained belief system. Who was he to turn their world upside down, and try to make them disbelieve? A believer in nothing, Bert could offer nothing of value as a substitute to make them want to go on living.

Bert figured he'd acquiesce long enough to find a way of escaping. But that plan changed when informed that HE was to light the funeral pyres which would hold the town's entire population. As they cooked, he was to read the sacred verses that guaranteed their quick entrance to heavenly mansions in the City of Gold.

Bert asked for privacy, then pondered the situation with cold objectivity. They wanted to burn. Who was he to deny their religious beliefs?

No doubt, many had money, baubles, bangles, and beads. After their demise, everything would be intact. He'd own a town with all its property and inventory. Not to mention all the cars, SUVs and trucks worth millions.

The enormity of his potential inheritance made his head spin. He, who was voted least likely to succeed in anything, was about to become disgustingly rich. All he had to do was light a match. One lousy match.

On the other hand, kids were involved. Was it murder to accede to the ardent wishes of religious zealots? If he refused and resisted too strongly, would they go crazy and torch him for not living up to religious obligations?

He'd do it.

He organized a gigantic funeral procession. All 2,341 residents of Wghaf assembled within a gigantic gasoline soaked tent, surrounded by a mountain of wood pilings.

Inserting earplugs, Bert lit a match. As the fire roared, he read aloud the silly jingles somebody'd called sacred texts.

Afterward, he felt hungry. Back at the restaurant, he warmed up a bowl of the fabulous chili he'd eaten for lunch.

"Bingo-dingo," he exclaimed, downing the first spoonful.

A CHINTZY CARPET

One evening, as Winston was stuffing a dead German into a back alley garbage can, a Portuguese barmaid stepped outside for fresh air. She screamed and ran back into the bar before he could shoot her with his silenced pistol.

After hearing his report, the station chief ordered Winston to disappear in the Casbah of Tangiers until things cooled down.

Winston hurried to the Lisbon Aerodrome to catch the night flight to Tangiers. While waiting for the eight-passenger, Ford Tri-motor airplane to depart, he decided to pass the time in the small, terminal cafe. The moment he entered, he scanned the room to see if any of the several dozen patrons were German agents. None of the faces matched any he'd memorized from dossier photos.

After downing two scotches, Winston was approached by an Arab wearing a business suit.

"Begging your pardon, Sir. You are English, no?"

"Yes, I'm English," Winston sniffed, while checking to see if anyone was looking his way.

"Permit me to introduce myself. I am Abu Yacob Ben Wadi, recently of Cairo. Now, sadly, a resident of Lisbon."

"Harry Ingram, London Times," Winston said, wishing the Arab would disappear.

Appearing nervous, the Arab wiped perspiration from his forehead with a grimy handkerchief. "If I may get directly to the point. Due to a slight misunderstanding, the police have confiscated my passport. Thus, I cannot leave Lisbon. But, I must get something to my son in Tangiers. You are going there, no?"

"Possibly."

"If so, perhaps you will deliver a parcel to my son. I am willing to give you this magnificent, two-carat ruby ring for your kind assistance. See how it catches the light?"

"A ruby to deliver a parcel? No thanks. I'm not interested in carrying contraband across any border. Not for a ruby ring, or all the gold in the Bank of England."

"You misunderstand, Sir," Ben Wadi said, wiping his forehead again. "Not contraband. A family heirloom. A small carpet."

"The post office offers reliable service. Certainly, they'd welcome your business, and charge far less than the price of a ruby ring."

"I do not trust the mail. This is worth far more than you can imagine. Let me show you." The Arab opened a case and removed a thin, chintzy carpet the size of a bath towel.

Winston had seen similar junk in bazaars all across North Africa. Why was delivering something so cheap and common worth a ruby ring? But those were strange times. Jews were giving fortunes for train rides to flee Nazi-held territories. And now Arabs were giving rubies for carpet deliveries.

"I will not withhold the truth," Ben Wadi said. This is a very unusual carpet. If one says, 'rise carpet,' it obeys. When one climbs onto the carpet and says 'go carpet,' he is taken anywhere in the world, in seconds."

"Perhaps you should use it to leave Lisbon and visit your son."

"I cannot. One is allowed to ride only thrice in a lifetime. Alas, I've used all three. But my son can use it for transport to South America. War is near. Europe, Asia, and Africa will not be safe. But the great ocean will keep South America safe. There, he will prosper. Here he will die. Please sir, take this carpet to him. Allah will bless you."

"How do you know I won't steal your carpet?"

"Allah would frown on such a monstrous sin, and send a thousand djinn to punish you severely."

Dammit! How the hell did they find me?This man's a loon. On the other hand, if I agree to deliver his crummy carpet, I'll be the new owner of that expensive-looking ring.

Winston asked for the son's address, took the ring and carpet, and boarded the plane.

The next morning, he put the carpet in a satchel and caught a cab. When he arrived at the blighted apartment building near the waterfront, he found the young Arab's quarters empty. Neighbors said he'd moved a week ago. Nobody knew where. Winston shrugged and headed back to his seedy hotel room in the heart of the Casbah.

That evening, while puffing an after dinner cigar in a shabby café, Winston felt eyes penetrating his back.

Turning, he saw an androgynous face of indeterminate nationality sitting with three thuggish-looking brutes.

"Mister Ingram. Are you enjoying Tangiers?" a voice purred in an accent he couldn't place.

"I don't believe I've had the pleasure—"

"Do not play games. I know what you have. I want it."

Winston chuckled. "You've mistaken me for someone else, Miss, uh, Sir. My name is Archibald Palmer. I have nothing of value, except my collection of African locusts, which is not for sale."

When the scowling goons reached inside their jacket pockets, Winston raced for the door. Jumping into a taxi, he headed for the Casbah. Certain they were following him, he switched cabs three times and gave drivers large tips for driving at breakneck speed through Tangiers' narrow streets. When he was certain his evasive tactics had worked, he returned to his hotel.

After a hot shower, he listened to BBC news on a battered radio. Prime Minister Chamberlain had just returned from Berlin. "Peace in our time," he told applauding masses after signing a peace treaty with Hitler.

Winston scoffed. He'd read highly secret intelligence reports about Hitler's global ambitions. He'd also read Winston Churchill's speeches in the *London Times* that warned against British complacency and appeasement policies. He agreed with Churchill that another European war was looming. He figured once it began, there'd be no safe haven for anyone in Europe, or Africa—especially intelligence agents. He knew that once war was declared, his life expectancy would be reduced to zero.

I'm getting too old for this, he murmured. The last war was horrible enough. If our intelligence is correct, Hitler's planning a war that'll make the last one seem like a bloody Boy Scout picnic.

He found himself wishing he were on the other side of the world on one of Tahiti's majestic beaches. Gentle Pacific breezes. Lovely Polynesian maidens. Peace and quiet. No Germans. No war. No espionage—ever again.

Someone knocked softly. "Mr. Ingram," said the voice from the café, "we have a business proposition."

Dammit! How the hell did they find me?

Grabbing a pistol, he pressed against a wall near the door. "I told you my locust collection is not for sale."

"Locusts do not interest us. We want the carpet. Just open the door slightly, pass it through, and you won't be harmed."

"What bloody carpet?"

"The one the Arab gave you. Before we killed him. The carpet that flies."

Who are they trying to kid? Something must be sewn inside that thing. Maybe it's filled with diamonds. Maybe Ben Wadi's a jewel thief, or deals in stolen gems. Why else would they threaten me over a chintzy carpet? "How much are you willing to pay?"

"We're not buying. We wish to trade. In trade for the carpet, we'll spare your life."

He wondered about the odds of a shoot-out. Even if he survived, he risked arrest, interrogation, identification. All hell would break loose among the twenty nations who jointly administered Tangiers, if they discovered his true occupation. They'd probably label him a dangerous provocateur, and charge him with instigating a destabilizing, international incident. If they didn't hang him, he'd rot in a stinking North African prison.

"I don't have the carpet." he called.

When they began to pick the lock, Winston felt panic rising. There was no way out, except through the window. But lack of a fire escape meant a four-story fall.

He figured he only had seconds left before they'd charge into his room. His mind raced. Then he remembered what the Arab said in the café about the carpet's magical properties. Desperate, Winston threw the carpet on the floor and shouted, "Get me the hell out of here!"

Nothing happened.

Dammit. What are the right words? He visualized the scene with the Arab and remembered Ben Wadi had used the words, "Rise carpet."

The moment Winston said those words, the carpet levitated a few feet.

Amazed, he grabbed his valise, climbed aboard, and yelled, "Go carpet!"

Instantly, Winston was hurled through the windowpane.

Seconds later, the door burst open.

While goons searched the hotel room, an Englishman rolled up a carpet and tucked it under his arm. Whistling "Rule Britannia," he strolled among coconut palms along a peaceful, moonlit beach.

JUNGLE ROT

"Do not go out tonight. The moon is full. Zombies will get you!"

Harry chuckled at the chambermaid's superstitions. "Better watch they don't get you first," he said, reaching toward her as if he'd suddenly become the Frankenstein Monster.

"You must take these things seriously, Mr. Stone. More goes on in Port Au Prince than any man knows—except the Prince of Darkness."

"I'm just going to Café L'Auberge, Bahody. It's only three blocks away. What can happen in three blocks?"

"Bad things happen in the blink of an eye in Haiti. My neighbor's chickens died last night. All four. One minute alive, the next—poof! A very bad omen. Listen. The drums speak of doom."

Harry heard ethereal percussion fading in and out with humid breezes. He refused give into the creepy feeling that suddenly struck. He knew it didn't pay to get the willies in Haiti. Once they took hold, they were hard to shake.

"Zombies are people who've been brainwashed to think they've died and resurrected," he said. "Threats of zombification keep people in line, and suppress crime in the jungle where police protection is nonexistent. Keeps jungle villages free of child molesters, rape, adultery, senseless killings. It's an interesting sociological phenomenon."

"Is that what they teach in America? If so, they teach lies."

"I must go, Bahody. Thanks for bringing tea and turning my bed down."

"Take this for good juju," she said. Her palm held an inch long, black fetish with red eyes. She blew on it three times, made gestures over it like a stage magician, and mumbled some mumbo jumbo. Giving it to Harry, she said it was blessed and would protect him.

Amused, He dropped it in his shirt pocket and left.

What he didn't tell Bahody was that he was about to meet a shaman at the café. From there they'd head for the bush where the shaman would demonstrate his powers.

On the way to the café, Harry saw enough strange people in the evening shadows to almost make him believe in zombies. Sallow-faced wretches leaned against blighted buildings, staring at nothing, saying nothing, doing nothing.

Following instructions received from the shaman's helper, he stopped at a vendor's hovel and bought three fresh eggs. The shaman had insisted he bring them for the demonstration.

Harry was looking forward to the foolishness. If it were entertaining enough, it might rate a paragraph or two in his book on Haitian folk rituals.

The shaman and his helper were waiting at a grubby outdoor table. If Harry hadn't had the willies before, he sure had them now. The man had a malevolent presence with laser eyes that seemed to penetrate Harry's psyche. Trying to look directly into them made him feel woozy.

The moment he sat down, the shaman began to relate embarrassing events from Harry's past. Harry had witnessed clairvoyance many times before, so he wasn't impressed. Nevertheless, the shaman's statements about how his parents died, and the circumstances of his divorce were accurate.

Getting down to business, the shaman told Harry to give his helper the hundred-dollar fee for the demonstration. Then he told Harry to pick a small object and it would be replicated within one of the eggs. Harry never heard that one before. He passed Bahody's black fetish. The shaman waved his hand over it, mumbled some words, and said, "It is done. A duplicate now sits inside one of your eggs."

Yeah, sure, Harry thought, returning the fetish to his pocket. *Pull that one off, and I'll give you a whole chapter in my book. Especially since you ain't getting near these eggs until the ritual begins.*

Minutes later, they left by rickety jeep for the shaman's jungle village.

The ceremony was definitely worth mentioning in Harry's book. The shaman danced and leapt like a crazed man to invoke a voodoo entity. When a spirit god possessed the shaman, Harry was amazed at the transformation. He'd seen ersatz and real possessions before, but this was the most theatrical.

With blazing eyes, roaring voice, and body quivering like a jellyfish, the new persona possessing the shaman demanded the eggs. When the helper placed them on the altar, the shaman filled his mouth with liquor, then spat on the eggs. Immediately, the intensity of drumming, chanting, and frantic dancing increased.

From several feet away, Harry watched the eggs very closely, expecting trickery. But nothing seemed amiss.

Worshippers danced frantically until they collapsed. When all were writhing on the ground, the shaman raised his arms and commanded, "Pick up the first egg and break it with your hands."

Harry did, and let the slippery mess drop to the ground.

"Pick up the second egg and break it with your hands."

Hard as he tried, Harry couldn't break the damn thing.

"As you see, you cannot break the egg. I have moved all the energy from your body to the egg. Take the egg with you when you leave here. Upon arising tomorrow, strike it with a hammer. Eat it raw. Then all your strength will return. Until then, do not lose or break the egg. If you do, your strength will be lost, forever. Now, I'll break the third egg and pour it into your hand."

When the shaman broke the egg, Harry almost jumped out of his skin. Inside the slimy yolk was a tiny replica of Bahody's black fetish. He'd seen enough. He wanted to get the hell out of there.

"Luzu will drive you back." The shaman clapped his hands sharply, shouting, "Luzu! Come!"

A short, native woman wearing tattered clothes came out of the jungle. She walked slowly, as if in a stupor. Her arms flopped at her sides.

"She looks drunk. I don't ride with drunk drivers," Harry said.

"She is not drunk. She is a zombie."

"What was her crime?"

"No crime. She is dead. Luzu, tell him."

"I...am...dead."

"I'm not going anywhere with someone who's in a hypnotic trance."

"Luzu is not in a trance. She is as awake as any zombie can ever be. She died, was buried, and was resurrected by me. She is one of the living dead."

"Bull! There's no such thing. You make people believe they're zombies to punish them for crimes. Even to enslave them. I'm not going anywhere with any of your brainwashed robots. I'll walk back."

"That would be foolish. The jungle is not safe. Many things prowl at night. Strange things. Evil things. You could be eaten alive."

"My fetish will protect me."

The shaman sneered. "That thing? It represents a fertility goddess of little consequence. It has no power here."

Harry turned to leave, but after a few steps lost his balance and fell. He found he couldn't get up.

"Have you forgotten? All your strength is within the egg," the shaman said. "For a hundred dollars, I will return it to your body. Wait! Your trousers are wet. You've smashed the egg!"

"Help me," Harry gasped. "I'll pay whatever you want."

"It cannot be done at any price. Your strength has spilled into the soil and cannot be collected. Soon, your eyes will darken, your body will turn to dust."

Luzu lay on the ground next to Harry. Embracing him, she kissed his mouth with cold, fetid lips. "Give him to me, Master. Make him a zombie. Let him walk with me in the twilight."

* * * *

Hundreds of zombies gathered to feast on jungle rot and witness the abominable yoking of Luzu and Harry by a possessed shaman.

Since then, every full moon, a zombie stares endlessly at a solitary patch of soil, somewhere deep in the Haitian jungle.

Some say he moans horribly.

Nobody knows why.

THE PINK CONTRACT

"Mister, would you like to buy some nice dreams? Only five cents each."

"You're selling dreams?"

"Yeah. Nice ones."

Unbelievable. So young and already a con artist. Talk about moxie!

What the hell, it was only five cents. And I liked her entrepreneurial spirit. Fishing in my pocket, I found a nickel.

"OK. I'll take one."

"Sign here, please," she said, pushing a clipboard toward me.

"Sign what?"

"This contract."

I laughed. This kid was something. She couldn't have been more than ten or eleven.

"I gotta sign a contract to buy something for a nickel?"

"Yeah. It's to protect both of us. Me especially, in case you wanna sue me."

"Why would I sue you?"

"After you have your nice dream, you might holler and say it could've been nicer. Then you might say it wasn't an honest deal and want your money back. I don't give refunds. That's why you might wanna sue me."

The kid was brilliant. I figured in twenty years, she'd be CEO of a multinational corporation.

"You wanna read the contract while I fill out your receipt?"

"Nah. I'd have to go and get my glasses to read all this tiny print. I trust you. I'll just sign."

I signed the bottom of a pink, 3 x 5 multipart form.

"Here's your copy of the contract," she said, "and here's your receipt."

The yellow receipt was half the size of the contract. She'd written my house number and, "1 each nice dream @ 5 cents per. Total: 5 cents. Paid in full. Cash." Her signature and the date were scribbled on the bottom.

"Thanks for your business, Mister. You've just bought yourself a nice dream."

"You're welcome. You're a very sharp girl. I think you're gonna be rich some day. Would you like a cold soda?"

"Sure."

I got a can of root beer from the fridge.

"Gee thanks, Mister. I'll make sure you have an extra nice dream. See you next week."

Next week? By then she'll have worked out a scheme to sell me ocean front property in the middle of the Sahara.

"You're coming back?"

"Yep. I'm gonna have a White Sale. Three nice dreams for a dime. One day only."

Her blonde pigtails were the same shade as my granddaughter's. But this kid had a nose for business. I'd have to tell the guys about her at tonight's poker game.

I mowed the lawn, had lunch, and watched a ballgame. Then, I must have dozed off.

I saw my boss pounding on his desk about a mistake I'd made. I saw myself standing in the unemployment line. Then suddenly, as if walking on stage, the little girl who sold nice dreams appeared.

"Here's your nice dream," she said.

A curtain parted.

I was looking through a store window at a magnificent Schwinn bicycle, loaded with shiny accessories. The one from my childhood. The one I'd always wanted, but could never have.

A man came out of the store and asked, "Are you Joey?"

"Yeah, I'm Joey."

"Well, today's your lucky day. You're the ten-thousandth person to look at that bike. You've won the contest."

I was thrilled.

Pushing the bike toward me, he said, "It's yours. Enjoy it."

I rolled it outside. Just as I was about to get on and take a ride...I woke up.

What a neat dream. Too bad I woke up before I got to ride that magnificent bicycle.

My lord! I just had a really nice dream. First in ages. Could it have been...? Nah.

Then I remembered how the girl had suddenly appeared in the dream.

Jumping into the car with a handful of nickels, I combed all the streets in the subdivision. But I couldn't find her.

A week later, she was at my door.

"How was your dream?"

"Nice. But it was over too fast."

"It's the length we agreed on."

"What do you mean agreed on?"

"Paragraph 7 of our contract says that nice dreams bought for five cents last for five minutes."

"Oh yeah," I said to cover my ignorance. I'd thrown the unread contract in the garbage.

"Do you want to buy a dream that lasts longer?"

"Is that a nickel extra?"

"No. Ten Dollars."

The kid was amazing. "You mean if I'd paid you ten more dollars my nice five cent dream would've been longer?" I thought wistfully about how neat it would've been to ride the bike in my dream.

"Yeah."

"But you didn't tell me."

"It's in paragraph 8 of our contract."

"Yeah. Paragraph 8. Well, you said you were gonna have a White Sale this week. Ten cents for three nice dreams. Here's three dimes. I wanna buy nine. So, how much longer will a dream last if I pay ten dollars?"

"An hour. It's in paragraph—"

"Right. Do you take checks?"

"No checks, no credit cards. Cash only."

"Wait here," I said.

I hurried inside and grabbed my monthly budget envelopes. Removed money from the one marked food.

"Here's ninety dollars cash. I wanna buy an hour's extra time for each of the nine dreams."

I figure it'd take her a while to write a detailed receipt. Meanwhile, I signed another of her contracts.

"Wait," I said. "Can I get any kind of dream I want?"

"Paragraph 12 says if you repeat some words while you're falling asleep, you'll dream about them."

"Like, if I say 'snow' and 'sleigh' over and over again, I'll have a dream about sleigh riding in the snow?"

"Yeah. A nice one."

Oh man. My mind raced trying to figure out what dreams I wanted. I could go back to the last Christmas my family ever spent together. An hour with them in a nice dream would be wonderful.

"Las Vegas" and "dice" could give an hour's worth of fabulous fun. Might even dream I won a million.

Then too, I could pair the words "beautiful model" and "bed." No telling where that one would lead for a whole hour. Maybe I'd repeat that dream two or three times. Damn! I could hardly wait for tonight.

Oh man. I could easily spend half my Social Security check on nice dreams, every month. At least I'd get something worthwhile for my money. I'd probably end up sleeping sounder, and living longer.

That night I could hardly wait to fall asleep. I repeated "beautiful model" and "bed" over and over again.

I was in Vietnam, caught in an ambush. An enemy soldier was about to thrust a bayonet into my chest. I woke up screaming.

What the hell happened? Once again, I repeated the model-bed sequence.

I was in the jungle, running for my life. A tiger was right behind me. I tripped. His teeth ripped into my face. I woke up yelling.

By morning, I was utterly exhausted.

That little brat rooked me. I didn't have a decent dream all night long.

During the rest of the week, I must have broken the world's record for anxiety dreams.

When she rang my doorbell, I barely made it to the door.

"You don't look good, Mister."

"You lied. I've had nothing but nightmares. I oughta sue you."

"You can't. Remember our contract? Tell you what I'll do. For a hundred dollars, I'll remove the jinx. Cash only."

I emptied my budget envelopes, and gave her the money.

"Why did you screw up my dreams?"

"I didn't. You did it yourself by not reading the contract."

"Oh hell. What paragraph?"

"Paragraph 1. It says, 'If you fail to say 'Cinderella' along with the other words, you'll have horrible dreams for a week.'"

"Why didn't you tell me?"

"It was in the first sentence of the contract. If you want me to teach you how to read a contract, it'll cost an extra fifty dollars."

I felt like choking the little twit.

"I guess you don't wanna buy nice dreams from me anymore."

"Right. Now get out of here. And don't come back."

"Don't you want to know the password, before I go?"

"What password?"

"Well, you still have nine nice dreams coming, with nine hours extra time to enjoy them. Cinderella was good only for the past week. You need a new one this week."

"What is it?"

"The contract says—"

"Just tell me how much, girlie, before I bop you."

"Since you're a good customer, twenty-five dollars."

I had to break my piggy bank to raise the money.

"Here. Now, what's the damn word?"

"Goldilocks. Want a receipt?"

"No!"

"Before I go, would you be interesting in some good luck coupons? Only five cents each."

PAYBACK

"This is intolerable!" the Haitian plantation owner yelled, while checking daily production figures for his zombie slaves.

"What is?" asked Boss Zombie.

"Last night Zombie 2058 cut only a ton of sugar cane. That's fifty percent below quota. Go find that slacker and bring him here. I think he needs a little bit of motivating." Cackling, the owner reached for a three-foot long syringe filled with murky yellow fluid.

"Yes, Master," said Boss Zombie.

Walking through the jungle in typical zombie style—arms extended fully outward, palms pointing to the ground, Boss Zombie's pop-eyes rolled from side to side looking for Zombie 2058.

Suddenly he heard someone singing. He would've turned his head in that direction, but zombies can't do that because of calcified neck muscles. Instead, he shifted his weight so his rotted feet twisted toward the sounds.

As he moved forward, he heard, "There's no business like show business like no business I know..."

"What the hell are you doing?" he hollered when he spotted Zombie 2058 hopping around on his only remaining, rotting leg.

"Tap dancing," 2058 said.

"What's tap dancing?"

"Something I saw people doing in the movies before I died. In one of them Fred Rogers and Ginger Astaire movies."

"Well, you better dance your way to the Master's mansion. He's angry. He says you've been slacking on the job. He says you need a bit of motivating."

"What's that mean?"

"You'll find out," Boss Zombie said, chuckling. "Let's just say that he's going to stick something in your eye."

"Will it hurt?"

"You bet your ass it will. Ooops you can't bet that—yours is gone."

"I don't wanna go."

"What? You can't refuse anything the Master commands."

"But I already did by slacking on the job. Look, I don't wanna cut cane anymore. It's a dead end job. I want more outta life. I wanna be a star!"

"What's a star?" asked Boss Zombie.

"Like Ginger Astaire and Fred Rogers were in the movies. People will come to hear me sing and watch me dance. They'll even pay money.

If they paid to see Judy Rooney and Mickey Garland, they'll pay to see me."

"That's stupid. Who would pay for such a thing?"

"Americans."

"You're crazy. They don't even believe in zombies."

"Not true. Look at this. It's a letter from New York. A famous producer wants me to audition for a part in a new Broadway show."

"I don't know what that is, but it sounds dumb." Grabbing Zombie 2058 in a chokehold, he said, "You're coming with me. The Master wants to see you now!"

2058 had anticipated a day such as this. He managed to break loose and shove Boss Zombie backward into a camouflaged, ten-foot deep pit that was filled with sharpened wooden stakes.

"You bastard!" Boss yelled when he realized he was impaled and couldn't move. "Help me get loose, or you'll be sorry."

Ignoring him, 2058 hobbled through the jungle toward the ocean. When he reached the beach, he dug up a canoe he'd stashed. Jumping in, he unfurled a BROADWAY OR BUST banner and began to row.

2058 made it to New York. His audition was successful.

Five years later, a very rich 2058 went back to his homeland for a visit.

The moment he entered the jungle in his expensive, custom-made suit, the plantation owner along with all the assembled zombie cane cutters applauded wildly.

"Welcome home," the owner said. "I saw clips from the Broadway show that you were in. I want you to know that I'm proud of you. I wish you would've have told me about your talents sooner."

"I'm glad you liked the show. And thanks for the wonderful welcome. Frankly, I thought you'd be mad."

"Why would I be mad?"

"Well, I used to be one of your slaves. And I hear it cost you $10,000 to turn my corpse into a zombie. I figured you wanted some payback."

"Payback? Nah. I'm willing to let bygones be bygones for a famous Broadway star," said the owner, extending his hand.

When 2058 clasped the owner's hand, the owner shoved him backward into a deep camouflaged pit filled with sharpened wooden stakes. It was the same pit 2058 had used to impale Boss Zombie.

Seeing a dozen stakes running through 2058, and that he was totally incapacitated, the plantation owner climbed down a ladder. When he reached bottom, Boss Zombie lowered a three-foot syringe.

Unable to move, 2058 saw the point of the dull, rusty needle inching toward his eye.

As the owner jammed the needle into 2058's eyeball and slammed the syringe to flood the zombie's head with murky yellow fluid, the victim broke into a song from the Broadway show, South Pacific.

"I'm gonna wash that man right outta my hair..."

He continued to sing, while the owner dismembered him with a chain saw.

The severed head continued singing Broadway tunes, as Boss Zombie shoveled lime into the pit.

* * * *

Though two years have passed, what's left of 2058's head continues to sing. Thousands of visitors to that part of the jungle have paid $20 each to put their ears against the soil to hear 2058's magnificent renditions of Broadway's greatest hits.

"Payback," a delighted plantation owner mumbles gleefully each time he sells a ticket.

GOOD HOUSE PETS

"Can I have a pet zombie for my fifteen birthday?" Billy asked his mom.

"No! Those horrible things eat people's brains. Do you wanna wake up one morning and find all your brains gone?"

"The ones they sell at Zip-Mart ain't like that," Billy said, showing her a newspaper ad.

She read aloud, "Domesticated zombies make wonderful house pets. Fresh shipment just received from Haiti. Perfect gift for teenagers. Get your pet zombies while they last. Just $29.95 each."

Billy's mom acquiesced and bought one for his birthday. Calling it Skip, Billy taught it to roll over, beg, fetch Frisbees. Skip slept under his bed.

One night, Skip jumped into Billy's bed, pressed against him and whispered, "I'm really a girl zombie. I can make you feel good all over."

"Really?"

"Sure. Wanna see?"

"Yeah!"

Billy's mom was alarmed when Billy didn't get up for breakfast. Knocking on his bedroom door, she hollered, "Wake up! You're gonna be late for school!"

When he didn't respond, she peeked inside. Blood and brains were smeared all over his pillow.

"I told you zombies eat human brains! But you wouldn't listen! Now look what happened! How the hell am I ever gonna get these stains out of your pillowcase?"

What happened to Billy was repeated 5,839 times that night across America.

Zip-Mart made a fortune selling blood-and-brains stain remover for pillowcases. Parents were upset when they discovered an ounce of stain remover cost twice the price of a pet zombie. On the other hand, the expenditure to remove the stains barely made a dent in the marvelous life insurance payments parents received for their massacred children.

At first many parents were dismayed. However, they soon realized having a fat wad of insurance money was far better than having a disobedient, insolent, slob of a teenager, who did nothing but destroy domestic tranquility.

Pet zombies became the hottest commodity in America. Parents bought, sold, traded, and rented them at an astonishing rate. Consequently, America's teenagers became extinct.

The Area 51 Option

With no more American teenage brains left to munch, all pet zombies headed for the nearest ocean, walked into the waves, and disappeared. Because they were never taught geography, they didn't know that Canada and Mexico existed and had several million teens available with ripe, tasty brains.

When CNN announced that pet zombies had suddenly disappeared from America, the world's parents urged Haiti to increase production. They mourned when the Haitian government announced that none were left, and no more could be produced. The illiterate witch doctor, who'd invented the pet zombie manufacturing process, had died before learning his ABC's and how to write. Thus, pet zombie recipes existed only in the witch doctor's decayed brain.

So far, every laboratory in the world has failed to replicate them to meet 1-billion back orders.

Until someone can devise a new way to create and mass-produce pet zombies, parents will have to put up with teenagers.

HARD LESSONS OF HISTORY

"Something's wrong with my hamster," Jim said to the veterinarian. "It's been growing bigger every day."

"How big is it?"

"Same size as my refrigerator."

"Sounds like a severe glandular disorder. Bring it to my office immediately."

"I'll be there soon as soon as I can get some neighbours to help me load it onto my truck."

When Jim arrived, the doctor told him to bring the hamster into the examination room.

"I can't," Jim said. "It takes six guys to lift him."

Grabbing his medical bag, the doc ran outside. "Good grief! It barely fits in the back of your truck."

The vet pressed his stethoscope against the hamster's side. "Geez. I never heard such racket. If I didn't know better, I'd swear I hear vehicles racing around inside your hamster. And the sound of marching soldiers."

"Can I listen?" Jim asked.

The vet passed the stethoscope.

"Hey, I hear helicopters! And ships blowing foghorns! What do you make of this, doctor?"

"I've seen several bizarre mutations lately. Three-eyed dogs. Ten-legged rabbits. But none had strange noises coming from inside their bodies. Something weird might be happening to your hamster's digestive system."

"Frankly, it sounds to me like an invasion force that's ready to launch an attack," Jim said.

"An invading army inside a hamster? C'mon, get a grip. Well, none of this makes sense. I'm going inside to confer with a colleague at the university. Maybe he'll know what's happening."

When the vet headed to his office, Jim thought he heard chainsaws. Checking his pet, he was amazed to see tiny chainsaws cutting small doorways through its fur from inside. The hamster acted as if nothing were happening.

Suddenly, tiny tanks and troops rushed out, blasting everything in their path. Attack helicopters slaughtered Jim. Tanks and cannons fired at the vet's building, blowing it to smithereens.

The same scene was repeated throughout the world. In three days, Earth was conquered.

"What are our losses?" the Emperor of Mars asked his conquering generals.

"Insignificant."

"Good. I'm glad you studied Earth's history very carefully. You were right when you said we shouldn't use wooden horses for our invasion, because that had already been done."

"Actually, it wouldn't have mattered, Your Highness. We've discovered that Earthlings do not study history anymore. We know more about their past than they do."

"To their great disadvantage," said the Emperor. "Too bad they didn't learn the hard lessons of history. Those who don't know the past are condemned to repeat it."

"Wonderfully wise saying, Your Highness."

"Thank you," the Emperor said. "Now, let's review our plans to invade the next planet. Tell me, do they have hamsters on Jupiter?"

A DEEP CUT

Robert saw an ad in the newspaper. "Loved Ones Returned. Minimal Cost. Why Be Alone?"

The next day, he sat in Madame Majestic's musty parlor.

"I miss my girlfriend," he said. I want her back, but she's dead. Can you bring her back?"

"Yes," Madame said. "I'll need a hundred dollars and a piece of her finger."

"I'd gladly dig up her grave right now and get it for you, but she's buried overseas."

"Then I'll need a piece of YOUR finger."

"When can you do this?" he asked.

"Now. Do you have the money?"

Robert gave her five twenties.

"Put your finger here," she said, pointing to a cutting board. "Bite hard on this sponge."

He'd never felt such horrendous pain.

"Drink this whiskey," she said, binding his wound. "It'll deaden the pain. Go home, turn off all the lights, and wait for her in bed. She'll come at midnight."

On the way home, he noticed the bandage was soaked and dripping blood. Alarmed, he stopped at a hospital.

"This is a nasty wound," said an emergency room doctor. "How'd you cut off the tip of your thumb?"

"The knife slipped when I was slicing meat."

"Frankly, this looks like a ritual cutting. I'll have to report this to the police."

Robert ran for the door, but slipped and crashed headfirst into a gurney.

Next thing he knew, he woke up in a hospital bed. Though dizzy, he went to the bathroom. The mirror showed a bandaged head. Then he remembered: Sandy was supposed to show up at his apartment at midnight.

Scrambling into his clothes, Robert bolted from the hospital, and floored his Mustang.

He managed to get into bed with only two minutes left. Trembling with sexual anticipation, he thought of the things they'd done so many times before she died. A year without her had made him ravenously hungry.

As the clock struck midnight, a glowing green mist appeared on the ceiling. It grew larger as it moved toward Robert.

"Sandy, my love," he called softly, when a face began to form, "I've missed you terribly." Closing his eyes, he spread his arms for her embrace.

When her soggy, cold lips pressed against his, he gagged from the stench. Pushing her away, he was startled to find he'd kissed a rotted corpse full of leaking cavities.

"Get outta here!" he screamed. "Go back where you came from!"

"It's too soon, my love. I'm yours until dawn. The only way I can return before then is to bring a sacrificial offering to the Gatekeeper of the Eternal Pit."

"What kind of sacrificial offering?"

"Your freshly butchered flesh."

"Take your piece of flesh," he said, spreading the fingers on his good hand. "Then get the hell outta here."

He shuddered when a cleaver appeared in her putrid hand.

Closing his eyes, he gritted his teeth and braced himself for the horrific shock. The chop came so swiftly, he didn't feel the slightest pain in his hand.

That's when he realized she'd chopped off something more precious than a finger.

M

When Martian hordes invaded, we fled to the forest.

"What will we do?" my sobbing wife asked.

"I don't know. I need to sleep a bit. When my mind's clear, I'll think on it. Did you have a chance to grab any food when we ran from the house?"

"Just this," she said, extending three cellophane-wrapped crackers.

"You eat them," I said.

"No, we'll share like we always have. Do you want your cracker and a half now?"

Hungry as I was, I declined. I'd save them for the morning. Dammit. How the hell am I gonna make it tomorrow on one-and-a-half saltine crackers?

"I wish it was safe enough to make a fire," Lisa said.

"But it ain't. Those bastards would be on us in a minute. Did you see all that green muck running from their mouths? Can you see yourself being covered with that slime as one of them is just about to toss you in its huge mouth?"

"Don't remind me. It's bad enough I had to see the neighbors being eaten by those monsters. I swear the sight will haunt me for the rest of my days. I hope I don't have nightmares about it. Dammit! I only have three sleeping pills left. I don't know how I'll be able to make it through the night once they're gone."

Then she started to scream.

I punched her to put her out. Dammit. Married 22 years, and never raised a hand to her. Now I had to deck her to save our lives.

Can't let myself feel guilty. I gotta hang on. If we're gonna survive for even a few days, I gotta have a clear mind. But I'm so tired after running for miles. Half the time I had to carry her, pull her, push her, to keep her going. I don't know how long we can last. No food. No water. Don't know where we can get any. Ain't even sure where we are.

I cradled her. I musta hit her pretty hard. Well, I did her a favor. At least her mind was peaceful for a while.

She woke. Rubbing her jar, she asked, "What happened?"

"You got dizzy all of a sudden and fell over. Before I could catch you, your face hit that boulder."

"It hurts. I wish I had some water to take some aspirins. Oh, Frank, what are we gonna do?"

"I just thought of something. We'll look for Morganites. I hear they keep six months worth of provisions in case of emergencies. I hear they got lots of guns too. Maybe I can get one from them and start fighting back."

"How are we gonna find them?" she asked.

"I don't know. But we'll find a way. Come to think of it, don't they paint big M's on their barns and roofs of their houses?"

"I never heard that."

"I heard it in a bar," I said. "So, when we get up tomorrow, we'll keep walking through this forest and look for Morganites. I'm sure they'll share their stuff with us. I have a few hundred in my wallet to buy stuff from them."

We spoke in hushed voices a while longer. Next thing I knew, it was dawn. I ate my crackers, then woke her.

We walked all day through the forest. Fortunately, we found a brook. Might have been contaminated, but we didn't care. We might not survive long enough for a bad infection to take hold.

As we approached the edge of the forest, Lisa said, "Look, there's a barn! Oh my God! It has a big M painted on the side."

"You sure? I can't see that far without my glasses."

"It's as clear as day," she said. She started to run.

"Stop," I hollered. "My knee hurts. I can't keep up with you."

"I'll run ahead and see if anybody's home," she yelled.

I called to her a few times to wait for me, but she didn't listen. She disappeared in a cornfield.

It was a while before I got to the cornfield. That's when the barn with the big M marked on the side came into focus. Lisa was right. I'm glad her eyesight was better than mine.

I felt hope rising for the first time in two days. Making my way through the cornstalks, I wondered if the Morganites had apple pie. I was dying for something sweet.

As I neared the end of the cornfield, I heard a blood-curdling scream. Looking between the stalks, I saw two Martians pulling Lisa apart and jamming her into their filthy, green dripping mouths.

Horrified, I fled back to the woods.

I didn't know which was worse: the hunger, depression, or terrible guilt I felt over Lisa's death. She never would have run to that barn if I hadn't told her how Morganites mark their buildings.

I had no idea Martians did the same thing.

HISTORICAL PERFORMANCE

Authorities in charge of New York City's annual Tap City Dance Festival were alarmed when they received a letter from lawyers representing the city's Monster Community. The monsters demanded the right to have 500 of their most talented zombies perform as tap dancers. What's more, they wanted the zombies to demonstrate their dancing talents in front of Fox News Studios on Fifth Avenue, so the entire world could see their performance on TV.

Alarmed at the implications of so many dancing corpses, and how that might impact the public's welfare, authorities denied the request. The letter to the city's Monster Community listed several undeniable facts:

- Zombies are dead people.
- They have a putrid stench.
- They eat human brains.
- They are always poorly dressed making themselves totally unpresentable to the general public.
- They scare children.
- Their rotting foot flesh might fall off during the performance and create horrendous public health problems.

The monsters sued. Their complaint charged city authorities with blatant discrimination. Especially since the tap dance celebration was formed to promote the virtues of community, individuality, and diversity, regardless of age, race, culture, gender, social, and economic background.

The monster's legal complaint said zombies represented both genders and all economic backgrounds. The mere lack of life was no excuse to deny them the right to perform on Manhattan's streets.

Judges ruled in favor of the zombies, saying the civil rights they'd enjoyed in life were still in force after death and zombification. However, judges added a caveat: the zombies would have to ride down Fifth Avenue on flatbed trucks, from which they would give their tap dancing demonstrations.

Fawning TV news reporters told the world round-the-clock about the upcoming zombie performance. Soon, millions of visitors arrived from every continent to witness the historical appearance of zombies at the annual Tap City Dance Festival.

Merchants were jubilant. Hotels were packed. Street vendors became rich overnight selling everything from hot chestnuts to Italian lemon ice.

On the day of the zombie performance, millions lined the entire length of Fifth Avenue. Precisely at noon, custom-built flatbed trucks left

Lower Manhattan. Aboard were 500 zombie tap dancers and 500 zombie accordionists.

Highly enthusiastic about their performance, the zombies danced so hard, chunks of flesh fell fall from their feet. Putrid bits and pieces flew into the crowds. But the crowds were so mesmerized, they didn't notice the bombardment of rotted, maggot-infested flesh.

By the time the truck arrived in front of Fox Studios, the zombies had danced so frantically, they were reduced to a legless mass. But that didn't lessen their enthusiasm. 500 legless zombies bounced up and down on their pelvic bones to the beat of 500 accordionists, who pounded their instruments so hard, their fingers were missing.

"Look, Mommy," said a kid watching TV in Australia. "Those people are playing accordions with their elbows."

The performance was so thoroughly enjoyed by all, the zombies were signed to dance in an upcoming Broadway musical. Not to be outdone, Hollywood began filming a musical, "The Zombies of OZ."

Flushed with success, the Monster Community promised to supply 1,000 zombies for New York City's annual St. Patrick's Day Parade. Participating zombies will mark the occasion by leaking Kelly-green goo from every body cavity, along the entire parade route.

A PREEMPTIVE STRIKE

The phone rang the moment I arrived home from the Tenth Annual Retired Police Detective Dinner.

"Pete DeSalvo," I said.

"I know your other name. The secret one the Irish government gave you," said a voice with an Irish accent.

"I don't know what the hell you're talking about." I slammed the phone down.

The phone rang again.

"Cut the crap!" I yelled. "Otherwise, I'll find you and bust your ass."

"O'Salvo. Please listen," the voice said.

That stopped me cold. How did he know the highest levels of the Irish Government called me by that name in their most sensitive reports?

Who the hell is this?" I growled.

"My name's Zack Dooley."

"How come you know the Irish version of my last name?"

"I'm a professional researcher. I was checking government archives in Ireland for a very important client. Saw your name on a hush-hush report. The one involving you and leprechauns."

"Dammit! That report was supposed to be sealed for seventy-five years," I said. "How come they let you see it?"

"Political connections. I read the part about how you got rid of all the leprechauns in Ireland twelve years ago. And how the Irish government renamed you O' Salvo to save face, just in case word leaked out. If their citizens ever found out a Sicilian-American, Los Angeles police detective cleaned up Ireland instead of an Irishman, there'd be insurrection."

"Dirty, rotten politicians!" I said.

"You got shafted," Dooley said. "When St. Patrick got rid of Ireland's snakes—which were nothing compared to leprechauns—they made him a saint. Now they drink green beer in his honor every St. Patrick's Day. Have they made you a saint? Have they named a day after you? What do they drink in your honor?"

"Nothing!" I yelled, kicking a chair.

"If you saved Ireland, why not do the same for your own country? At least Americans treat their heroes like royalty. They'll put your name on cereal boxes, tennis shoes, freeways."

"What the hell are you talking about?"

"A monster's loose in Los Angeles. You gotta find it and kill it."

"I haven't heard about any monsters in town," I snapped.

"My neighbor saw it on Wilshire Boulevard last night," Dooley said. "He said it looks just like the Frankenstein monster from the movies."

"He's nuts. Frankenstein's a fictional character. He never existed."

"Frankenstein used to be a fictional character," Dooley said, "but not any more."

"Whadda ya mean?"

"Some goofballs managed to patch together a bunch of body parts and create a monster that looks just like the movie Frankenstein. They even brought it to life. Remember that big power outage that affected the whole U.S. last year?"

"You mean the one they blamed on UFOs?"

"Yeah. I heard it had nothing to do with UFOs," Dooley said. "It happened because the nation's entire electrical output was used to create a gigantic burst of energy—to bring Frankenstein to life. They succeeded. And now he's prowling Los Angeles. It's only a matter of time before he starts invading schools, churches, golf courses, crack houses, and kills everybody in sight. Nobody will be safe."

"Nonsense. Universal is probably making a monster movie. Maybe the guy playing Frankenstein didn't have time to remove all his make up. Hey, I'm busy. Tell the cops. Don't call me again!"

Making a salami sandwich, I recalled how I saved an ungrateful Ireland from the scourge of leprechauns. The little creeps were responsible for committing countless petty crimes. When I discovered they were planning to expand to Los Angeles, I went to Ireland and wasted the bastards in a preemptive strike. Wiped out over a million of them. Irish radicals screamed, "Genocide." Then they posted a million dollar reward for the head of whoever did it. I hoped those loons would never find out I was the culprit.

That afternoon, I watched a double-header on TV. Between innings, the camera scanned fans sitting in the stands. It paused on the face of a good-looking woman for a few seconds, then moved to the guy sitting next to her. He had the kind of face that haunted people's dreams.

Sonovabitch! He looks like Frankenstein!

He was talking on a cell phone and laughing. I made a mental note of the section number.

I figured he was Frankenstein about as much as I was the Wolfman. He probably wasn't half the size of a movie Frankenstein. My gut told me he was a freakin' leprechaun in disguise. Only a leprechaun would be nutty enough to run around imitating a movie monster. But, how the hell did he escape my dragnet in Ireland? Why is he in Los Angeles? Are people too zonked to notice?

I decided to kill him the same way I wiped out his brothers—with a compact flamethrower that fit inside a student back pack.

As I packed the flamethrower, I added two Molotov cocktails. They came in handy in Ireland when I found leprechauns at the ends of rainbows. I'd toss a Molotov cocktail into the woods, which would create a roaring forest fire. That's how I smoked out all those little green freaks hiding in bushes. When they tried to escape, I blasted them with my flamethrower.

I was on the freeway and heading for the ballpark to assassinate the phony Frankenstein when Dooley called again.

"Please don't hang up," he said. "I have important new information about Frankenstein. He was spotted at the ballgame."

"I know. I was watching the game on TV. He's sitting next to a good-looking woman."

"Thank goodness you finally believe me. I hear noise in the background. Where are you?"

"On my way to kill the bastard."

"Fantastic!" Dooley said. "I wanna be there when you do it. Let's meet at the snack bar closest to his seat."

"No. I'm gonna rush in, zap him, and get the hell outta there before anybody has a chance to react."

"But if I'm there when it happens, I can record everything on my camcorder. I should be able to sell the images to CNN for big bucks. I'll split the take with you, fifty-fifty."

"Sounds like a good plan," I said. "Meet me there. What are you wearing?"

"Green shirt, white shorts."

Arriving at the ballpark, I headed for the snack area. Halfway there, my gut nagged me. I wondered why Dooley was so hot on getting Frankenstein wiped out, and why he avoided telling the cops. Plus, he didn't ask what I was wearing, which meant he already knew what I looked like. Maybe he had me under surveillance.

I called a friend who had a computer.

"Hey, Harry. It's DeSalvo. Do me a favor. Google on the name, Zack Dooley, and the word researcher.

I heard fingers tapping on keys.

"He's a member of LAGL," Harry said.

"What's that?"

"Leprechaun Anti-Genocide League. A political fringe group. Says here they're offering a million bucks for the head of whoever killed Ireland's leprechauns."

It was all a setup. I figured the world's last leprechaun was running around LA posing as Frankenstein just to attract my attention. Dooley was a radical nut trying to snag me for killing Ireland's leprechauns. He was trying to smoke me out into the open. He probably sent his leprechaun buddy posing as Frankenstein to the ball game, and slipped a TV cameraman some bucks to get Frankenstein's face on TV. He must've done it to force a confrontation between me, him, and Frankenstein. Then Dooley would shoot me on the spot with a pistol disguised as a camcorder. He'd chop my head off and take it to Ireland to collect the million-dollar reward from his radical pals.

No way was I gonna meet Dooley at the snack bar. I headed directly to the stands.

When I found the section and walked toward Frankenstein, he stood and cheered. Just as I thought! The bastard was half the size of a Frankenstein movie monster. Beside that, his skin had a slight, greenish tint found only in leprechauns.

Putting on dark glasses, I pulled my baseball cap down to shield my face. Walking past him, I hollered something in Gaelic that no Irishman or leprechaun could possibly resist: "Free beer at the snack bar!"

In a flash, Frankenstein elbowed me out of the way, and raced toward the snack bar. I followed him.

He hollered to somebody in a green shirt and white shorts standing by the snack bar. I figured it was Dooley. Both yelled at the guys behind the counter, "Where's the free beer?"

I got both of them with a single Molotov cocktail.

I managed to get out of the parking lot before homicide cops erected barricades. Then I took back streets all the way home.

I opened a beer and pondered the day's events. That's when the phone rang.

A man with an Irish accent yelled, "Dracula's alive! He was spotted last night at Malibu!"

I SHALL RETURN

Japanese flak shot out the controls of my fighter plane. I went into a steep dive. My plane shattered when the Pacific rose to meet it. Don't know how deep I plunged.

"Mom!" I yelled. Then nothing.

"Joey, I got fresh baked bread and homemade butter," said a familiar voice. "And ice cold chocolate milk. Your favorites. Come this way and have all you want."

"Grandma? Is that you? Where are you?"

"Over here. Hurry while the bread's still hot."

"Wait, Joey, come this way," said a second voice. "Let's play hide-n-seek."

"Stevie?"

"Yeah. I'm over here. Try to find me."

How wonderful to hear Stevie's voice again. My favorite cousin. My partner in bike riding, roller-skating, mischief-making.

"Watch out for cars, Stevie," I called. "Your mom still cries for you."

I felt pulled in two directions. On one side were Grandma's hands, full of tantalizing bread, butter, and chocolate milk. On the other was a misted forest with Stevie.

"Grandma, can you wait until I play with Stevie?"

"After twelve years, a few more minutes won't matter," she said.

"Stevie, after I find you, let's go skating...."

Gagging. Coughing. Spitting.

Ocean waves. Rustling palms. Hot sun.

Nausea rippled through my gut. I threw up.

How the hell did I get on this beach?

It was late afternoon when I had enough strength to push myself up. I staggered toward the jungle's edge. When my eyes focused, I saw a campfire. The breeze pushed odors of frying fish my way.

"Hey! Whoever's there. Help me."

No answer.

I managed to crawl to the fire.

The fish was delicious. So was the open can of crushed pineapple. I drank from coconut shells filled with fresh, chilled water. Surprisingly, one contained ice cold Coca Cola.

Saw a pack of cigarettes. General MacArthur's picture and, "I Shall Return" were on the side of the pack.

Puffing away, I lay on my back surveying the stars. Then, the full reality of what'd happened, struck me, and I began to shake. Thank goodness I was alive. But where was I? Did anybody back at the base know I'd survived?

I'd ask my benefactor about everything, tomorrow. I owed him my life. Some thanks I'd shown him by raiding his dinner and gobbling everything. I'd make amends tomorrow.

So good to know the island was populated. Maybe a crashed pilot. Gotta be American, what, with Lucky Strike cigarettes, Del Monte Pineapple, and Coca Cola.

Feeling somewhat comforted, I fell asleep.

I woke up a distance from where I originally lay the night before. Did I sleepwalk? Was this the psychological aftermath of a horrendous crash?

Following my footsteps on the beach, I returned to where I'd dined. I saw canned bread, Corn Flakes, powdered milk, sugar, powdered eggs, juice, smokes, cooking tools, and a fresh fire.

After whipping up breakfast for two, I yelled, "How do you like your powdered eggs? Green, or burnt?"

Figured I'd hear a good-natured laugh, and jungle brush crunching as he headed my way. But nobody responded.

I looked around the small island. Didn't find a soul. "Hey, Buddy," I called over and over again, to no avail.

I hid in the bush, hoping to glimpse my provider. Whenever I did, the fire and meals showed up elsewhere.

After several days, I tried to figure how to get rescued. Didn't dare build a fire at night. The enemy would send patrol boats to bombard the place. I sure as hell didn't want to be taken prisoner or get killed after all I'd gone through.

On the other hand, why be in a hurry? This was an island paradise.

Once rescued, they'd give me a physical, maybe a few days off, and put me be back patrolling the skies over New Guinea. Might even get shot down again.

Then I chided myself. This was war to the death. They needed every hotshot pilot they could get. I had to find a way back.

On the tenth day, I saw a black mass toward the horizon. Scared me. I hid in the jungle.

Talk about relief. It was one of our destroyers. Sailors in a skiff headed my way. I ran like hell to greet them.

Maybe it was delayed shock. But once the doc checked me out in sickbay, I slept on and off for three days.

"Who saved you?" the doc asked.

"Don't know."

"Where'd all the provisions come from?"

"I have no idea."

"You absolutely sure there aren't any natives on that island?"

"I don't think so. I looked every day. Didn't see a soul. By the way, how'd you know where to find me?"

"You'd never believe me. Doesn't matter. You're here and in good health. You'll be back in the air in no time."

* * * *

The Base Commander sent for me.

"The King of all the islands wants to see you," he said.

"Why?"

"He wants to see the pilot who was rescued from the ocean. I'm surprised, because he has refused to meet with any Americans since we occupied this island. Well, go see him. Take this bottle of bourbon. Tell him it's a gift of respect from me. Tell him that I too am a chief, but not nearly as great as he is. Maybe that'll flatter him enough so that he'll decide to meet me. I'd like to recruit some of his men as coast watchers."

Two days later, four islanders arrived carrying a chair decorated with orchids and mounted on wooden struts. They lowered it so I could board. While carrying me to their village, they sang haunting melodies.

Arriving at the village, they placed the chair on a flower-covered path. Two gorgeous women took my hands, and led me to the largest hut in the village. Once inside, a middle-aged man in magnificent robes approached.

"So you are the pilot beloved by the Gods," the King said, circling me, pinching my arm, as if testing to ensure I was human.

"I don't understand your meaning, Your Highness."

"The dolphins told our fishermen about you. How you fell from the sky. How they saved you. How they fed you with things they gathered from sunken warships. Where they'd taken you. Our fishermen told your Navy."

"Dolphins?" I didn't dare laugh at his superstitious stupidity.

"Oh yes. You are beloved of the dolphins, and more so by the God of the Dolphins."

"Why would the God of the Dolphins love me, your Highness?"

"Perhaps he has found your sacrifices pleasing."

"But I don't worship any god."

"Perhaps it is time to start. What is there to lose? After all, you have been given a second chance."

To humor the old King, I agreed.

Then I had a strange dream.

From then on, I took a pile of gum and chocolate bars on every mission. On my return, I'd fly as low as possible and toss them into the waves. One particularly large dolphin would hurl himself up so high I'd catch him on my wing.

I'd open my canopy, and we'd speak of many things.

THE CONTRACT

"I'm a sour old bastard suffering from crushing loneliness," cried Nessie.

"I understand your pain," Harry yelled through a bullhorn. "But, you're uglier than sin. Those humps on your back are grotesque. If you weren't so mangy-looking, you wouldn't be lonely."

"It's not my fault I was born this way. Why wasn't I born a beautiful butterfly instead of the Loch Ness Monster?"

"Blame it on Fate," Harry said.

"Do you realize they wouldn't even give me a part in Jurassic Park? Broke my heart. I told them I'd work for minimum wages. I figured if kids saw me in the movie, they'd realize how nice I am. Maybe they'd ask me to come to their schools for show and tell. But the director wouldn't have it."

"Why?"

"Well, the actors got fed on the set as part of their contracts. The director said I was so huge, they'd spend almost their whole production budget just to feed me."

"If you'd didn't hide in this loch so much, especially when explorers show up, you might get some good press coverage."

"Why don't you take me home with you? You come here every week to see me. You always stand way up on a hill as if you're scared of me. I don't eat people. I eat algae. If you're so worried about my welfare, why don't you build a lake behind your house, put me there, and I'll live happily ever after. You could even sell tickets so people could come to see me."

"Great idea! I'll go home right now and prepare a contract. I'll be back in a few hours."

"Wonderful!" Nessie exclaimed, shedding joyful tears. "I won't hafta be lonely anymore."

Harry prepared a contract stating he'd get 99% of the proceeds from ticket sales, snacks, and Loch Ness Monster merchandise. He'd tell Nessie that it was a 50-50 deal. She'd never realize he was cheating her. It would never occur to her to ask a lawyer to review the contract. She was a gullible, uneducated dullard who'd believe anything. Scottish taxpayers were to blame. They'd refused to pay for the construction of classrooms the size of dirigible hangars to accommodate her.

Rushing back with the contract, Harry called through the bullhorn. Nessie rose to the surface immediately.

"Here's the contract. No need to read it," he said, knowing she was illiterate. "I'm gonna climb down to the shore. I tied a pen to this broomstick. I'll put it in your mouth so you can wiggle your head and make your mark. That'll make the contract legal. And I brought a camcorder to record this, so I'll have proof that you really signed."

Nessie giggled with excitement as he approached. She bowed her head so he could place the broomstick between her incisors.

When he disappeared, Nessie burped loudly.

"Work's every time!" she chuckled, as she descended to her lair for an after dinner nap.

RAZZLE-DAZZLE

Harry went into Ye Olde Curio Shop and slammed an antique bottle on the counter.

"Nothing in this place is any damn good!" he shouted.

"What's the problem?" asked the gnomish old shopkeeper.

"Remember last week when I rented a wishing bottle, and it turned out to be empty?"

"Right. And I gave you this one as a replacement. So, what's the problem now?"

"I only got two wishes. The genie owes me two more."

"You must've done something wrong. Did you talk nice to her like I told you?"

"Sure did. Every time I made a wish, I said pretty please with chocolate syrup on top. For the first two wishes, everything worked out fine. She brought me a hundred billion in cash, and the German castle I always wanted."

"Well, maybe you should count your blessings," the shopkeeper said. "You have enough money to last a lifetime of fantastic luxury, and you have a fine new home. How many bathrooms does it have?"

"Don't change the subject. I have two more wishes coming. If I don't get them immediately, I want half my rental fee refunded."

"Frankly I never heard of a genie failing to carry out a customer's wishes."

"Well, this one did. Just as I was making my third wish, she interrupted me right in the middle of the sentence."

"Hmm. That's highly irregular. What did she say?"

"That she wanted a pepperoni pizza. With extra cheese. I wondered what the hell was going on? Since when does a genie get on her high horse and order me around? It's supposed to be the other way around. And I told her so."

"What did she say to that?"

"No pizza, no wish. I asked her why she wanted pizza at a time like this. Do you know what she said to me?"

"I can't imagine."

"I've been cooped up in bottles for 5,000 years, and I'm famished. Get me a large pepperoni pizza, or no third wish. So, I called Pizza Hut and had them deliver one. Would you believe that tiny thing ate the whole thing? She didn't even offer me a slice. Then, she made me wait until she took a nap. Plus, I had to sit there and listen to her burping while she snoozed."

"I assure you I'll report this to the Genie Supply Warehouse," said the shopkeeper. "You can be certain she'll be strongly reprimanded."

"Serves her right. But there's more. When she woke up, I tried again. I said, 'Oh beautiful magical genie, I wish for all the oil in the Middle East be placed in the ground under my castle, pretty please with chocolate syrup on top."

"And?"

"She just sat inside the bottle with her arms crossed, looking pissed. 'What's the problem now?' I asked. Know what she said to me?"

"I'm afraid to ask."

"She said from now on, she wants me to say, pretty please with chocolate syrup, marshmallow, peanuts, whipped cream, and a cherry on top. So, I told her that's not the magic formula, and that she's just stalling. I told her to get the oil like I just wished for. But she wouldn't budge. She took out a marking pen, a piece of cardboard, and made a sign that said ON STRIKE. You can see it taped to the inside of the bottle."

The shopkeeper examined the bottle. "That's awful. I'm going to call the Genie Supply Warehouse right now."

Grabbing his cell phone the shopkeeper dialed. "Hello...Customer Service? I got a problem. A very irate customer's in my shop, and he's complaining about one of your genies. What's her name? I'm checking the bottom of the bottle now. It's Razzle-Dazzle. Oh, I see. Well, that explains it."

"What did they say?" asked Harry.

"She's a defective model. They shipped her accidentally. They said I should swap this bottle for another. Only problem is, all my genie-filled wish bottles are rented. None are due back until a week from Tuesday."

"That's OK," Harry said. "By then, oil will be up to $200 a barrel."

Before leaving, Harry picked up the bottle. "Hey genie. You know, I think you are the most beautiful female I've ever seen. My fourth wish after you got the oil was gonna be that you became a full sized woman. Then I would've married you, and we could've had a fabulous time together living in my castle, spending my money, and selling oil to the world. Wouldn't that have been better than living in stupid bottles for the next gazillion years? Imagine all the pepperoni pizzas you could've had."

The genie smiled, tore up the sign, and said, "Your wish has been granted. Not only has all the oil in the Middle East just been relocated to the land under your castle, but I also threw in every drop that the United States has offshore. Plus the deposits in Anwar, Alaska. Now make your wish, because your offer about making me a real woman and helping you spend all that money sounds fantastic."

"Can't," Harry said.

"Why not?"

"I'm on strike."

GRAND ENTRANCE

"Dora, the other members of the team and I have decided that you should have the magnificent honor of being the first person to enter King Gazanga's tomb. Congratulations!"

"No way! Just because I'm the only women on this team, doesn't mean I'm gonna do everything you ask. Hell, I've cooked all the meals in this miserable desert for you guys. And I've lost more than my share of sleep on night watches, making sure jackals and bandits didn't attack while you guys snored. But here's where I draw the line. Why don't you do it? Or Harry? Or Nick? Or any of the other guys?"

"For goodness sakes! You make it sound like we're trying to punish you. What do you think we are—a bunch of misogynists? This is a fantastic honor we're bestowing on you as a reward for all your wonderful support. You'll go down in history as the first woman ever to break the seal of an ancient Egyptian tomb and go inside. Oprah will break her neck to get you on her show. You'll be the darling of CNN, Fox News, not to mention every woman's organization around the world. The President will invite you to the White House. And that's just for starters."

"Hmm. Does sound pretty good," Dora said.

"Your life will change forever. You'll be a hero. Imagine what it'll be like when Random House offers you two million to sign a book contract. Think of all the girls who'll look up to you. Mothers will name their daughters after you. So will high schools. And maybe even a couple of parks. You'll be the toast of Washington, New York, Hollywood. So, take this sledge hammer, hit that door to break the seal, and march right into that tomb."

"What about the nasty curse? It says he who breaks this seal will be attacked by giant praying mantises, after his head splits wide open from being struck by lightening. And the ground will open and swallow what's left of him. And his miserable carcass will fall into the Pit of Fire. And he will suffer excruciating pain from horrible burns for all eternity—not to mention the constant sting of worms nibbling away at his innards."

"You can't possibly believe that. When you translated the hieroglyphics on the door, didn't you say it used the words he and his?"

"Yes."

"How can those words apply to you? You're a her. It didn't say her carcass would burn, or get munched by worms. So take this sledgehammer and whack that door."

"Will you guys take lotsa pictures to prove I did it?"

"Of course. We'll sell them to National Geographic for a bundle. Hey Nick, is the camcorder ready?"

"Yeah," Nick hollered.

"What about the rest of you guys. Are your digital cameras ready?"

All replied positively.

"OK, Nick, start your camera the minute she picks up the sledgehammer."

Dora grabbed the tool. "Damn, this is heavy."

"Say something for the camera," Nick said.

"What should I say?" she asked.

"Describe what this is all about and what you're doing."

"Hello everybody. I'm Dora Duncan. I'm a senior majoring in Archaeology at Santa Buffoona University in California. I'm carrying this sledgehammer, because I've been selected by Dr. Brown and his archaeological team, to break the seal of King Gazanga's tomb. Hi Mom! Hi Uncle Harry!"

"Speed up a bit," Brown said. "I'd like to get inside that tomb before sunset."

Walking faster, Dora added, "I want to thank some people, who in their own ways, made this day possible. The first is the guy at the candy store who told me to stay in school when I got preggers at fourteen and almost quit. Then there's the guys at Joe's Bar for teaching me what life was really all about, and—"

"Please save that for another time." Brown said. "How about describing what you see as you approach the entrance."

"It's sandy around here," Dora said. "This is, after all, the Sahara Desert. And the Sahara is known to be pretty sandy. And even though this is a desert, there's lotsa Egyptian Desert Pigeons. Oops. One of them just dropped something on my head. Nick, can you get a close up of my hair so people can see how different their gunk is from American pigeons?"

"Don't loose track of what you're doing," Brown said. "Keep focused on the tomb."

"The tomb's just a few feet away," Dora said. "It has a wooden door. Imagine a bunch of Egyptian carpenters from 75,000 years ago using their ancient tools, trying to make an ornate door. They musta suffered terribly in this horrible heat while they—"

Breaking into song, she warbled, "Tote that barge...lift that bale...get a little drunk and you lands in jail." Then she added in her normal voice, "Makes me wonder how their union let them put up with such intolerable working conditions. The bosses could've had this door made in Suez where it's a lot cooler. Just goes to show how management exploits labor every chance it gets."

She stopped three feet from the door.

"Well here it is. And here I am. And here's the sledgehammer. So now, I'm gonna raise this ugly old thing and hit that door. I've always wondered why tools always have to be so ugly? Why don't they paint them pink once in a while? Or lavender?"

"Hit the damn door, already," Brown said.

Dora swung with all her might. The door gave way, breaking the seal.

The entire team applauded and cheered wildly.

Lightening and giant praying mantises prevented Dora from hearing their accolades.

BLUEBERRY PIE

Anybody who goes to Roswell looking for evidence of an alien landing is stupid. Nothing happened there. It was a fabrication. But the lie's been repeated millions of times since then, and most people believe flying saucers landed in Roswell sixty-one years ago. What jerks.

I know it's all a bunch of hooey, because the freakin' things landed in my wheat fields. And I live in Texas, about 300 miles from Roswell.

No little green men were involved like the newspapers and radio said. They were orange. And they weren't men. They were aliens.

I got the first one with my rifle. When it jammed, got the second with my hunting knife. Buried the Martians in my fields. If they were Martians. No telling what they were.

As to the saucers, they were the size of tractors. Both disappeared the very night the things landed. Maybe their alien buddies came and got them.

After killing one with my knife, I wiped its blue blood—or whatever it was—on a handkerchief. The stain smelled pretty good. Taking it to Lawton's Drug Store, I showed it to old man Lawton. Asked him what he thought the stain was.

"Paint," he said without looking close.

"Paint don't smell like this," I said. "Take a sniff."

"Don't need to. I can smell the blueberry pie stain from here.

"What if I told you it was Martian blood."

"I'm a busy man, Frank. I don't have time for jokes."

"Just wanted to see how you'd react if I said it came from a Martian, considering all the wacky news coming from Roswell about them saucers and little green men."

"Mass hysteria," Lawton said. "An invention of idle minds. All those Army Air Force guys came back from the greatest and most exciting war in history. And now, with nobody to fight, they're bored to death. Maybe they'll get a crack at the Russians soon, now that the Red Army's gobbling Eastern Europe. In the meantime, the guys stationed at Roswell gotta come up with another enemy until they have to slug it out with the Russians. But the new enemy's got to be more exotic than the Red Army. Something that's tougher to beat. So, they decided to make up a story about invading Martians."

When I left Lawton, I figured it best I buried the handkerchief and knife. Nobody would've believed me back then if I told the truth. They were too wrapped up in Roswell.

* * * *

After sixty-one years, the baloney about aliens is far thicker. Druggies hallucinate about being abducted by aliens. We've put men on the Moon and reconnaissance vehicles on Mars. Funny how none of those vehicles have spotted any green aliens. Or grays. Or oranges, like those that stepped out of saucers in my fields.

Far stranger things than my blue-stained, blueberry pie-smelling handkerchief are offered by Internet sites these days. If I offered it for auction, I suspect few would bid. My handkerchief can't match grilled cheese sandwiches imprinted with the face of God. Nor can it hold a candle to stolen communion wafers consecrated by the Pope.

The fact that my handkerchief still smells like blueberry pie might make it even less desirable. They might say I added something to make it smell good.

On the other hand, I could use more money to keep up with the rising cost of gas and medicine. I thought about exhuming the remains of the two aliens I killed back in 1947—if anything is still left—and offering them on eBay. I'd tell the truth. Give the whole story.

The day I was gonna open the graves, I heard something on Fox News that changed my mind. The commentator told of something super-spectacular offered on eBay. When I heard what it was, I figured it made no sense to dig up alien remains and try to compete.

Not when the Shroud of Turin was offered with no reserve and a starting bid of one dollar.

FIRST DAY OF SCHOOL

"Help! Somebody call 911!"

"What's the problem?" Percy Pepper called to the woman running toward him, clutching a small boy.

"There's a blue gorilla in the kindergarten room! It's jumping up and down on the teacher's desk!"

Gorilla screams echoed throughout the school.

"Don't be alarmed. I'm the principal. I assure you everything's OK. How about a nice cup of tea? Perhaps your son would like a donut."

"But what about the gorilla?"

"I'll have Security check the room."

Pepper mumbled something into a phone. "That should take care of it. By the way, I'm Percy Pepper."

"I'm Snowbird Snodgrass."

"Welcome to Rasputin Elementary School. You and your son are the first to arrive. Did you know this is an award-winning elementary school?"

"That's nice. But what about the blue gorilla?"

"Well, sometimes we misinterpret what we see."

"You trying to tell me I didn't see a blue gorilla?"

"You saw a gorilla, but she's not blue. She's indigo. Miz Gruntz would be deeply offended if she knew you called her blue."

"Miz Gruntz? Is she the school mascot or something?"

"Not exactly," he said.

Pepper's phone rang.

"That was our security patrol. Everything's fine. Miz Gruntz just wanted a banana."

"Why is the gorilla, er, Miz Gruntz offended if somebody calls her blue?" Snowbird asked.

"It's political. She comes from Gruntonia, which was partitioned by the Amalgamated Nations back in 1955. North Gruntonia is populated by illiterate, headhunting blue gorillas. Miz Gruntz comes from South Gruntonia, which is populated by indigo gorillas. They're affluent, well educated, and speak English fluently. Calling a southern gorilla 'blue' is considered vile hate speech in Gruntonia."

"Geez. I didn't know," Snowbird said.

"I'm bored," the kid whined. "I wanna see the gorilla again."

"Can your son have a donut?"

"Sure. If it's free."

"What's your name, Sonny?"

"Jaws."

"What a nice name. Were you named after your dad?"

"Nope."

"I named him after the big shark in the movies," Showbird exclaimed.

"Jaws, how about sitting in the secretary's office while I talk to your mom?" Pepper said. "I'll give you a nice coloring book and crayons. And two jelly donuts."

"What kind of coloring book?" she asked. "I hope it don't have no cartoon characters. They scare him somethin' awful."

"I'll give him the one he'll use in Kindergarten. Don't worry. It doesn't have any weird cartoon characters. This one has very nice pictures of North American serial killers and their victims. He'll love it."

Pepper ushered the boy into the secretary's office and closed the door.

"Feeling better?" he asked, as Snowbird noisily sucked her tea.

"Kinda. You sure that gorilla won't run in here and attack us? I thought they were dangerous?"

"Oh no," Pepper chuckled. "The Santa Buffoona school board would never hire anybody dangerous. Miz Gruntz is our new kindergarten teacher. Being a quintuple minority, she fits the bill very nicely. Plus, she adds incredible diversity. There's strength in diversity. Now our school will be stronger, better, more wonderful. You're for diversity, aren't you?"

"With all my heart and soul. But she's still a gorilla."

"A most refined and civilized creature," Pepper assured. "She comes from the most famous gorilla family on Kong Island. Her father is the first of his species to win a Global Peace Prize. He's also Southern Gruntonia's representative to the Amalgamated Nations."

"Oh, wow," Snowbird cooed.

"They say he'll probably be their next Secretary General."

"You mean my Jawsy will be taught by somebody whose daddy will be top dog of the Amalgamated Nations?"

"More like top gorilla. Isn't it fabulous?"

"Thrilling," Snowbird said, eyes glowing.

Loud roaring and chest thumping came from the direction of the kindergarten. Snowbird and Pepper pretended they didn't hear.

"As Miz Gruntz's pupil, your son will learn all about indigo gorilla culture. Did you know they're the missing evolutionary link between animals and humans?"

"No I didn't."

"In fact, Indigo gorillas may even be more human than we are. You believe in evolution, don't you?"

"I guess."

"Never doubt it. Our ancestors were apes and gorillas. That makes Miz Gruntz, family. So your child will be taught by a family member."

"I guess it's like having my great-great-great-great grandma, from way before Adam and Eve, coming here to teach," Snowbird said.

"Exactly."

"I feel much better now."

"Let's go to the classroom, and I'll introduce you."

"Great!"

On the way, Pepper explained the wonders of diversity and cultural equivalence.

Opening the classroom door, they saw Miz Gruntz swinging from one ceiling light fixture to another. A double summersault landed her directly in front of Snowbird and Jaws.

The gorilla sniffed them from head to toe. Pointing at Jaws, she said, "He smells like jelly donuts."

Gruntz's melodic, English-accented voice so thoroughly charmed Snowbird, she almost curtsied.

Suddenly, the gorilla grabbed Jaws and tossed him headfirst through a window. "I hate the smell of jelly donuts!" it screeched, frantically jumping up and down on the bloody corpse.

"Get away from my son, you ugly blue gorilla!" Snowbird screamed, pounding Miz Gruntz with both fists.

The gorilla stepped away from the mangled blob. "Did you hear what she just called me, Principal Pepper?"

"I certainly did. Disgusting. I warned her about that."

"Do I have to take this kind of hate speech from parents?"

"Absolutely not."

The gorilla broke Snowbird into a dozen pieces, while Pepper called the janitor for a cleanup.

"Principal Pepper," Gruntz called, while chewing on Snowbird's thumb, "would you care to join me for breakfast? Or would you prefer we wait until the children arrive and share this delicious fare with them?"

"Let's wait. We can make this an instructional event, a profound learning experience. I can hardly wait to see the look on all those young, eager faces when they get their first taste of cultural diversity."

THE CHERRY BOMB

Artie was so furious when ants infested the chocolate cake at their Memorial Day picnic, he vowed vengeance. He told his three cousins what happened.

"Let's find out where the bastards live," Billy said, "and wreck the place."

"How are we gonna do that?" asked Chucky.

"We can use this cherry bomb," said Danny.

All agreed, except Chucky. He liked ants. Especially after his mom told him how hard they worked. He figured ants were far better than his dad, who was always drunk and jobless. Refusing to participate in the ant massacre, he stayed behind.

Artie, Billy, and Danny followed the line of ants into the woods. While they searched for the anthill, Billy said, "My dad told me that somebody killed an elephant in the Bronx Zoo with a cherry bomb. Blood and guts were all over the place for a whole mile. Just think what it'll do to a bunch of crummy ants."

"It'll be like an atomic bomb," Danny said.

"Look," Artie said, "there's the anthill."

The boys didn't know that a civil war had recently ended between two ant factions. The winners formed the world's first ant republic. They ratified a constitution and held presidential elections. Their new President had been sworn in that very morning.

Had the kids looked carefully through a powerful magnifying glass, they would have noticed tuxedoed and beautifully gowned ants entering the anthill to attend the Inaugural Ball. And had they examined ants coming from the picnic, they would have noticed their waiter uniforms and the chocolate cake morsels they'd brought for the Inaugural Banquet.

Artie placed the cherry bomb on top of the anthill. Billy adjusted the bomb to make sure it was directly over the entrance. Danny lit the fuse.

Countless celebrating ants died. Ant blood and guts were strewn for a mile. Some of it fell on Chucky's head as he sat at the picnic table. Wiping off the gunk, he noticed it consisted of bloody heads, arms, legs, and guts. He wept over the carnage.

Though temporarily disoriented by the surprise attack and horrendous damage, the Ant Intelligence Network, AIN, sprang into action. They summoned their vast network of secret informants.

That night, a million AIN agents invaded every boy's bedroom in town. They dusted the boys' fingers for traces of firecracker gunpowder. Considering 1,320 boys lived in town, they figured the task would take all night. However during the first hour, the AIN Director sent a message ordering all his agents to drop what they were doing and converge on the apartments occupied by Artie, Billy, and Danny.

When dusted with AIN's forensic chemicals, the boys' fingers turned electric blue. This wouldn't have happened if they'd obeyed their mothers and washed their hands before going to bed.

Before sunrise, Artie, Bill, and Danny exploded simultaneously. Their blood and guts were spread everywhere for a mile.

Everybody wondered how such a horrible thing could happen to three, cute kids.

But the ants knew. They too had cherry bombs in their arsenals. Using their legendary strength and vast numbers, they'd rolled a cherry bomb into each boy's mouth, while he slept.

****

Sixty years later, Chucky's great-grandchildren asked him to tell them scary stories, as they sat around a campfire. He told them the one about the guy who blew up an elephant with a cherry bomb. They squealed with pleasure when they heard how blood and guts were strewn for a mile in all directions. The kids enjoyed the story so much, they clamored for more. Chucky then told them about his three cousins who'd suffered the same fate at the hands of the Ant Intelligence Network.

The kids didn't believe him.

Until he showed the citations and medals he received from AIN for squealing on his three cousins.

RED DUST

The priest sensed a profound change of atmosphere the moment someone entered the darkened confessional. Gripping his pectoral cross, he blessed himself, and mumbled prayers of protection in Latin. He'd encountered dreadful phenomena during his forty years as a missionary in the Haitian jungle, but none darker than this.

Opening the sliding panel to expose the metal grill that separated their faces, he noticed a peculiar odor. *The stink of Hell*, he thought, blessing himself again. *Another* ***dark entity*** *sent to harass me.* He quickly unscrewed the top on a small bottle of holy water.

"Why are you here?" he asked.

"I'm so happy, I could burst," said a woman's voice. "I just wanted to tell somebody."

"This is not a place of levity. This is a confessional. A place where evil is purged."

"I thought priests were bound to listen to anybody in a confessional, no matter what they had to say."

"You heard wrong. Tell me what you have to say. Make it quick."

"Suppose I buy your time. Say, five minutes worth. For that, I'll put $1,000 in the poor box before I leave."

"Don't bother to lie. Evil can do nothing good."

"Evil is good fun," she said. "More than you could ever imagine."

"Your mind is foul."

"How true. Do you know what I am?"

"Vampire."

"Verrry good. How did you know?"

"I can smell it on you."

"Ah. A holy man who can discern essences. Let me ask you, Holy Man, have you ever bitten into a neck and drunk your fill?"

"It's a stupid question," he said.

"Hardly. It's a life changing experience. It's so erotically satisfying, nothing else approaches it. You may be celibate, but I'll bet you deeply crave erotic adventures."

"We're not here to talk about me. Get to the point."

"I just wanted to tell you how happy I am. I can barely contain myself."

"How many victims fell into your clutches tonight?" he asked.

"Fifteen. Five an hour. I've achieved a record. I know the Master will richly reward me for being so wickedly industrious. Would you like to be the sixteenth?"

"One false move, and you'll regret coming here," he said, gripping the bottle of holy water. "Listen, don't wait until Judgment Day. Confess everything now and ask for the Almighty's forgiveness. The fact that you were able to enter this holy place without bursting into flames shows you can yet be saved. Confess your foul murders. Ask forgiveness. Amend your life. Do it quickly."

"No! I love my existence. I feel bliss throughout my waking hours, and even more so at night. But you have to wait until you're dead, and then hope you'll attain the bliss of Heaven—a place my Master assures me doesn't exist. Even if it did, why wait? Join me now. I could use a priest for an ally. You'd make a good decoy to ensnare trusting souls."

The priest hurled holy water through the screen. She didn't even have time to scream.

Using his cell phone, he called the housekeeper and asked her to put a fresh bag into the vacuum cleaner and bring it to the confessional.

Later, when opening the bag and examining the deceased's dust, he found it bright red. He carefully poured her dust into an empty Coke bottle. Sealing it with wax, he said prayers of exorcism.

Carrying the bottle to the cellar, he stored it in a safe next to others containing werewolf, ghoul, and zombie dust. Then he called an all-night radio talk show that focused on the uncanny and macabre.

"I just killed a vampire," he told the host.

"Sure you did. And I guess you see black helicopters, shape-shifters, and were abducted by aliens."

"You must listen to me very carefully. The only reason I'm telling you this is to warn everyone. Beware! This kind is particularly vicious. Like nothing seen for hundreds of years."

"Oh? How can you tell?" asked the host.

"She turned to red dust."

"Really? And what color dust is there when you kill vampires that aren't as nasty?"

"Grey."

"I see. So, what did you do with the red dust?"

"I vacuumed it. Then I poured it into a Coke bottle."

"Hear that folks? Here's a guy who kills vampires and stuffs them into Coke bottles. What about zombies? Kill any of those lately?"

"As a matter of fact I did. But that was in Haiti a few months ago."

"Oh my. Aren't you the nasty serial monster killer. How about telling us what color zombie dust is."

"It depends on how they were zombified. But most are pale yellow."

"Get the hell off the phone, you freakin' loon, and go take your meds!"

Later that night before returning to his coffin, the talk show host took inventory—just in case the goofy caller had actually killed a vampire. Checking the seventeen coffins hidden beneath his Beverly Hills mansion, he found one empty. One of his newest female recruits hadn't returned from her nightly hunt, and dawn was near. There was no time to search for her remains and perform a resurrection ritual. He raged and pounded the walls.

With only minutes left before the accursed sunrise, he summoned rats, lizards, lice, beetles, leaches, and cockroaches. He ordered them to scour every nook and cranny of the city for a sealed Coke bottle containing red dust. Whoever found the bottle would be awarded a dozen putrefied corpses on which to snack. An even richer reward awaited the one who found the vampire killer.

Closing his coffin lid, he fell asleep wondering why the killer chose a Coke bottle instead of Pepsi.

THE SPIRITS KNOW ALL

Facing foreclosure on their house, Jim and Lisa consulted a Spirits Know All Fortune Telling Board to see if their luck would change. When it said they'd win a million dollars in the lottery in three days, they were ecstatic.

"Is there anything else we should know?" asked Lisa, as their hands rested on the planchette.

The planchette spelled out: WARNING.

"What's the warning?"

WIN BIG LOSE BIG.

"Whadda ya think that means?" she asked Jim.

"Who cares? In three days we're gonna be rich! Ya-hoo!"

"Do you believe everything it told us tonight?"

"Yep," Jim said. "A guy at Smitty's Bar uses this board all the time. The spirits said he'd win a red Lexus convertible in two weeks. And it happened."

"Did he mention anything spooky?"

"Whadda ya mean?"

"Somebody said using this board lets evil spirits in the house. And once they get in, it's hard to get rid of them."

"Superstitious nonsense!" Jim exclaimed.

Next morning at breakfast, Billy, their six year old asked, "Where's Gitmo, Daddy?"

"In Cuba."

"Is that far away?"

"Yep."

"I was there last night," Billy said.

"You mean you dreamed about being there," Lisa said.

"No. I was really there."

"Oh my, what an imagination. So what were you doing there?"

"Helping to waterboard some bad guys."

Startled, Jim asked, "Why'd you do that?"

"Sergeant LeHate said it was the only way to get them to talk."

"Who's he?"

"Pulling a three-inch, green plastic soldier from his pajama pocket, Billy added, "This is Sergeant LeHate."

Jim and Lisa chuckled.

That afternoon, Billy's kindergarten teacher called Lisa at work to relate a shocking incident. A box of crayons was missing from the classroom. When the teacher asked who took them, nobody answered. But Billy said he'd find out by waterboarding everybody in the classroom.

Though deeply perplexed, Lisa and Jim figured if they ignored Billy's fantasies, they'd quickly dissipate.

Next morning, Lisa and Jim were shocked to see scratches on Billy's face.

"How'd that happen?" she asked.

"I fell during bayonet practice in Afghanistan."

"I see," said Jim. "And I suppose you and Sgt. LeHate were there last night."

"Yep."

Jim, who'd served in the National Guard said, "Make believe this broom's a rifle with a bayonet, and my easy chair's a bad guy. Show me how you'd attack him."

Jim was astounded when Billy assumed the correct posture, raced toward the chair, let out an ear-piercing yell, and thrust the broomstick into the upholstery. Unnerved by the demonstration, Jim called a psychiatrist.

"Sounds like a normal boy with a rich imagination," the doctor said. "Don't be so anxious. At his age, these things pass quickly."

"But how could he know about waterboarding, and Afghanistan?"

"Probably heard it on TV. News stations mention those things endlessly. As for the bayonet, he probably saw how it's done while watching war movies. However, if he starts to act out his fantasies bring him to my office."

Next morning, Billy limped to the breakfast table. His mom shrieked when she saw his blistered, bleeding feet. They rushed him to a hospital emergency room.

"How'd this happen," asked a doctor.

"Me and Sergeant LeHate were on a forced march last night," Billy said. "It was worth it. We caught up to the enemy and killed them all."

The doctor recommended a psychiatrist. Jim mentioned he'd already consulted one.

That night Jim and Lisa won a million dollars in the state lottery. To celebrate they ordered a super deluxe pizza and a six-pack of imported beer.

Filling Jim's glass, she said, "Remember what the Spirits Know All Board told us?"

"Yep. It was right about us winning big time!" Jim replied.

"I was talking about the other thing it said. About winning big and losing big. Listen...I have a funny feeling. I want you to keep watch over Billy for a while. Then when you come to bed, we'll really celebrate."

Jim let himself into Billy's room, and headed for the closet. Keeping the door slightly ajar, he sipped beer while his eyes adjusted to the dim glow of a night light.

Before long a glowing green mist entering Billy's room. Out of the mist stepped a six-foot, plastic soldier in full combat gear, carrying two assault rifles.

Aghast, Jim saw Billy jump out of bed and snap to attention.

Handing Billy a rifle, the soldier barked, "Here's tonight's orders: we'll attack a stronghold north of Baghdad. But first we have to liquidate a spy."

The soldier threw open the closet door, and pointed to Jim. "Shoot this rotten spy!"

"But that's my dad."

"Shoot him now!"

Billy raised his rifle.

"Don't do it, Billy" Jim yelled, wetting his pants.

"Kill him, or I'll drop your ass in the middle of a terrorist camp without a weapon!" the soldier shouted.

When Billy hesitated, the soldier grabbed him and started to spin. Suddenly Billy and the soldier disappeared.

Frantic, Jim called 911. Nobody believed his story.

He called the FBI and Homeland Security hotlines. Both agencies warned him about harsh penalties for perpetrating hoaxes.

Next, he tried a radio talk show.

"Hear that, folks?" said the show's host. "We got another alien abduction by a green meanie. But this one looks like a soldier and is made outta plastic. Sounds like this goofus forgot to take his meds."

At her wits end, Lisa said, "Let's ask the spirits. They'll know what happened."

Their hands shook as the planchette sped across the Spirits Know All Fortune Telling Board.

"Why is it spelling HAMS?" she asked.

"I don't know."

They asked again where Billy was. This time the answer was HAMAS.

"Oh no!" Jim screamed. "Hamas is the most vicious terrorist group in the Middle East."

While Jim was on the floor trying to revive Lisa, the planchette spelled out on its own: WIN BIG LOSE BIG.

GOT MILK?

When high winds and a blinding snowstorm came, so did the zombies.

Stands to reason. If we get cold, so do they.

I wondered if one showed up, was I obligated to extend charity and compassion?

As I pondered this metaphysical question, one crashed through the door of my mountain cabin.

"Brains," he said, heading toward me with outstretched arms.

"Hold it," I shouted. "Is that the full extent of your vocabulary?"

That stopped him cold. Looking at me through lifeless eyes, he gurgled something unintelligible through his decaying throat.

"It's no wonder you guys haven't gotten anywhere in the world. Your English skills are so severely limited. Same with your range of socially acceptable behaviors. Even worse is your diet. Do you realize what you're missing?"

Another gurgle.

"I bet you've never been on a swing. Or a rollercoaster. And I'll bet you've never experienced the simple joys of munching chocolate chip cookies."

His arms were still outstretched, as if reaching for my neck, but he hadn't moved an inch. I thought perhaps my words had stirred something deep inside his calcified brain. Maybe for the first time in his miserable, zombified existence he was beginning to question who he was, where he was, why he was there, and what life was all about.

"Come, sit," I said, pointing to a chair. "I just made a fresh batch of chocolate chip cookies. Try one. I'm certain you'll like it. Even if you don't, it'll expand your culinary horizons."

Though I didn't expect him to respond, he took a seat with arms still outstretched.

"Try to put your arms down," I said gently. The moment I uttered those words, I was struck with a most powerful intuition. Maybe the position of his arms had something to do with his eating habits. The practical side of my brain immediately scoffed at such a strange idea. And yet, I was intrigued.

"Do you mind if I try to lower one of your arms?"

No response.

"Okay, I'm gonna get closer. And I'm gonna press on your arm. I'm gonna ask you not to bite my head while I'm doing it. Promise?"

No response.

Sometimes in life, you have to take risks to achieve a noble goal. I edged closer. And closer. And closer still.

He grunted.

I can't say I wasn't scared. But then so were Charles Lindbergh, Christopher Columbus, not to mention cave dwellers who first discovered fire. Struggling to overcome my fears, I put my hands on his forearm and pushed down.

His joints squeaked, as I pressed harder. When I gave it all I had, his arm fell into his lap.

"Cookies," he said.

Damn! I was right! A raised, extended arm was somehow mysteriously tied into his dietary cravings. I almost wept at the thought of how many years these poor creatures had been so vastly misunderstood, mistreated, malnourished. Maybe this one was taking his first baby steps toward a remarkable career. Maybe one day he'd even become an astronaut. Thoughts of adoption filled my head.

"I'm going to try to lower your other arm."

When I did, he said, "Milk."

"Good boy!" I exclaimed, patting him on the back.

I put a warm chocolate chip cookie in one of his hands and a cold glass of milk in the other.

He didn't react.

"Eat cookie," I said, grabbing one and munching on it. I figured if monkeys and apes could imitate human behavior, so could this large beast.

But nothing happened.

I poured milk for myself and took a swig.

"Drink milk," I said.

When he didn't, I yelled, "Stupid, dumb-ass zombie! Even freakin' monkeys can do what I just showed you."

Just as quickly, I chastised myself for being so harsh on this snow-covered, frozen, pitiful being.

"Okay, I'll help you," I said. I broke a piece from a cookie and rubbed it against his gray, mottled lips. "Open wide."

He did.

I pushed the piece into a putrid mouth that reeked of decaying jungle rot.

That's when he bit my fingers off. Even worse, he jumped out of his chair and bit my head.

Next thing I knew, he screamed and fled the cabin into the freezing night.

Three broken zombie teeth were on the floor.

It was the first time in my life that I ever appreciated the titanium plate surgeons had inserted into my cranium after a terrible motorcycle accident.

* * * *

I learned several things from this episode:

- Zombies are craftier than we think.

- They don't give a damn about cookies or milk.

- If you're gonna try to put something into a zombie's mouth, wear a suit of armor. Or, have a nasty motorcycle accident so you can get a titanium plate put into your head. Especially in the area where zombies like to bite.

THE ANNIVERSARY PARTY

Cool Pacific breezes woke Marcia from a chloroform-induced stupor. She moaned when she realized she was tied to a wooden chair. "Where am I?" she mumbled.

"On the beach at Bodega Bay," said Henry.

"Why am I tied up?"

"To make sure you attend the anniversary party."

"For who?"

"To celebrate the fabulous movie that was released fifty years ago."

"Let me go, Henry. You're acting crazy again."

"Just relax and enjoy the party."

"But nobody's here. And where is the food?"

"Tied to a chair," he said.

"Does this have something to do with your favorite movie, Alfred Hitchcock's *Psycho*? Are you making believe you're that loon, Norman Bates? So who am I...his mother? Or the woman he stabbed in the shower?"

"It's not about *Psycho*. Otherwise you'd be tied up in a motel room shower. Besides, that's not my favorite movie."

"OK," she said, "you had your fun. Untie me and let's find a nice restaurant. My treat. Then we can fool around. Whadda ya say? These ropes are hurting me."

"But if I let you loose, you'll miss the party. And you'll nag me about that like you do about everything else."

Ignoring her protests, Henry poured a jug of honey over her head. It ran down her face and over her shoulders.

"Stop it, you lunatic! I'm getting sticky all over! Dammit! You musta forgot to take your meds again!"

"Nag, nag, nag," Henry said, as he opened a bag and poured the contents over her head.

"Ow. It's getting in my eyes. What is this?"

"Bird seed."

"Let me go right now! I promise I won't tell the cops or your psychiatrist. Let me jump in the bay to clean this stuff off. Then I'll make you feel real good. For as many times as you want."

"I can't let you go. I promised them you'd be here for their anniversary party."

"Who's them? Are you seeing little green men again?"

"Something better," he chuckled.

Henry put a birdcall between his lips and blew hard.

"What are you doing?"

"Calling our guests. Look...here they come." Henry raced for the safety of his car, as swarms of squawking birds dived toward them. Landing on the beach, they surrounded Marcia.

Henry was startled when none of the birds approached her.

A seagull flew toward Henry's car. Landing on the hood, he motioned for Henry to lower the window.

"What's going on?" the seagull asked.

"I'm having an anniversary party for you guys."

"Why?"

"To celebrate the release of my favorite movie fifty years ago."

"Which one?"

"*The Birds* by Alfred Hitchcock."

"Never heard of it. Let me check with the guys to see if any of them ever did."

The seagull flew to the birds, squawked a few times, then returned to Henry's car.

"None of the guys ever heard of that movie," said the seagull. "What's it about?"

"How a bunch of birds went nuts and attacked people. Even little kids. It happened right here at Bodega Bay. It was scary. And very bloody."

"Sounds goofy," the seagull said. "None of us would ever dream of doing such a crazy thing. By the way, what kind of bird is that tied to the chair?"

"That's a woman, not a bird."

"You sure?"

"Of course I'm sure."

"Hmm. I could swear I saw her flying around San Francisco last week. Well, we'll be on our way. Have a nice day."

"Aren't you gonna eat the dinner I put out for you and your friends?" Henry asked.

"What dinner?"

"The one tied to the chair."

"Nah. We're all on diets. Besides, we're not cannibals."

"Hold on, you freakin' jerk! I spent time, effort, and money to prepare this special anniversary dinner for you guys. And now you tell me you won't eat it? That's a damn insult!" Henry pulled a pistol from the glove compartment and blew the seagull's head off.

The birds scattered when they heard the gunshot and saw their friend fall to the ground.

The sudden recognition of what he'd done jolted Henry back to reality. He ran to Marcia and untied her. Told her he was just fooling around, that he meant no harm.

Delighted to be free, she jumped into the bay and cleaned herself.

Dripping wet and sitting in the car she said, "You never told me what your favorite movie was. The one you wanted to celebrate."

"*The Birds*," he said.

"Never heard of it."

"It was that fantastic Alfred Hitchcock movie. The one where a bunch of birds went nuts and started attacking people. Even little kids. It happened right here in Bodega Bay."

"Sounds goofy," she said. "None of us would ever dream of doing such a crazy thing."

"That's exactly what the seagull said. Wait a minute. What do you mean by saying 'us?'"

Marcia slammed Henry's head against the steering wheel. After dragging his unconscious body onto the beach, she made a call on her cell phone.

"Hi Gramps. Did you ever hear of the movie, *The Birds*?"

"Sure did. I was in it. I played a crazed seagull that tore the flesh off an old lady's face. You shoulda heard her scream. Best fun I ever had. Why do you ask?"

Marcia explained.

"By golly, Henry was right about having an anniversary party. I'll round up a bunch of gulls and sandpipers who were in that movie. We'll be there in an hour."

Henry woke to find he was naked and tied to the chair. The birds that gathered around him drew lots to see who'd get first taste. Marcia won. She rammed into Henry's face with all her might. The birds cheered wildly when they saw Henry's eye impaled on her beak.

"Happy Anniversary!" the old-timers shouted. Then they finished what they started in a movie fifty years ago.

A WONDERFUL GIFT

Joe and Bill were watching Monday Night Football when somebody knocked on the door.

Opening the door, Joe was startled to see a huge gorilla in a delivery uniform. Next to him was a purple refrigerator wrapped in yellow ribbon and topped with a big bow.

"Sign here," said the gorilla.

"Who's it from?" Joe asked.

"I don't know. There's a card attached."

Pulling the card from the refrigerator, Joe opened it and read aloud. "A Gift Just For You." The card was unsigned.

"Where do you want this thing?"

"Put it in the kitchen."

The gorilla grabbed the refrigerator, slung it under his arm, and carried it into Joe's kitchen.

"Thanks," Joe said.

The gorilla put out his hand, and waited. Joe gave him five dollars. The gorilla threw the money, roared ferociously, and jumped up and down.

Bill ran into the kitchen. "Give him a banana before he tears your place apart!"

Grabbing two bananas, Joe offered them to the gorilla.

The gorilla stopped his tantrum immediately. Grabbing the bananas, he said, "Have a nice day." A second later, he was gone.

"What the hell was that all about?" Joe asked.

"Blame it on outsourcing," Bill said. "Consider yourself lucky it spoke English." Then he added, "Geez, I never saw a purple refrigerator before. Where'd it come from?"

"I don't know. Whoever sent it didn't sign the card. I'm gonna open it. If somebody was nice enough to buy me a gift like this, maybe they were nice enough to put something valuable inside."

Joe cut the ribbon, and opened the refrigerator. Instead of shelves, he found a second door inside made of old, weathered wood. Mounted on the door was a red flashing neon sign that said: KELLY'S BAR.

Astonished, Joe opened the wooden door. Suddenly, the apartment was flooded with loud music, raucous laughter, and the odor of stale beer.

"Sounds like somebody's having one helluva party in there."

"Let me have a look," said Bill.

"There's nothing to see. It's pitch black inside."

A voice rang out from inside the bar. "Close the damn door! You're lettin' flies in!"

Startled, Joe slammed the wooden door shut.

"Don't open it again!" Bill hollered. "It could be the doorway to Hell."

"How can that be Hell when everybody's having such a great time?"

The door flew open on its own. A woman's voice called, "Hey, Handsome. Come inside and join the party. I'll buy you a beer."

"Did you hear that?" Joe asked. "She sounds hot. Hey, if a babe wants to buy me a beer, I sure ain't gonna disappoint her."

"Don't go!" Bill said. "She could be one of them hags I heard about on a spooky talk show. They look great for a while, then when you're in their clutches, they turn into ugly, man-eating monsters."

"That's bull. I'm going in."

Bill jumped in front of the door. "I swear, if you try to go in there, I'll bust your head."

"Move away or you're a dead man!" Joe yelled.

Suddenly, Kelly's door swung outward with such force it knocked Bill over. Huge pointed claws reached out, grabbed his ankles, and yanked him into the darkness.

Though Joe tried to save Bill, he wasn't quick enough. The door slammed in his face. Hard as he tried, he couldn't open it. He ran to the garage, grabbed a sledgehammer, and slammed the wooden door with all his might. But he didn't even make a dent.

Dialing 911, he hollered, "Help! This is an emergency! Something weird just pulled my friend inside a refrigerator. And I can't get the door open."

"Is it a purple refrigerator?"

"Yeah."

"Was it delivered by a gorilla?"

"Right."

While the operator said, "I'll hafta put you on hold—the same thing's happening all over town," sharp claws grabbed Joe's ankles and pulled him into the darkness.

RAH-RAH-SHISH-BOOM-SNAKE

The sound of pounding drums was manic, horrific. Vibrations pierced the fifth floor of the university library, penetrating Joe's entire being.

Dammit! Another interruption. First it was a bunch of ditsy dames at the next table, who kept giggling. Next, a maintenance jerk spent ten minutes drilling something by the elevator. Then a buzzing, math study group parked themselves nearby. Joe moved three times so he could study for his Religion and Anthropology final. Now he had to contend with a bunch of wild drummers making a racket from which there was no escape.

Peering out a window, he saw nothing. Where was the noise coming from? He hadn't seen a notice anywhere about a Saturday morning rally. Who the hell would be in a rah-rah mood anyway, on a chilly December morning?

Fifteen minutes passed without letup. Joe swore it sounded like recordings of frantic voodoo drums he'd heard in class. Were Haitian visitors plying their trade in broad daylight, substituting the jungle of downtown redevelopment for the Haitian bush?

He decided to investigate. Once outside, the noise was head splitting. Vibrations bounced off every surface, every pore.

Fast-walking five blocks, Joe turned a corner and beheld a spectacular scene. The Snake God. Worshippers. Sacrificial offerings. Frenzied dancers. Spirited drummers. A pagan pep rally right in the middle of the city.

He'd forgotten the city was erecting a statue to honor the Snake God, placing it exactly where, in past generations, the city's Nativity scene had always stood. This was the day of welcome for the ancient deity: a black coiled snake, the god of blood lust and human sacrifice.

Realizing he was witnessing something from the pages of his Religion and Anthropology textbook, Joe tried to push through the crowd for a closer look. He didn't get far. Believers kept curiosity seekers at bay. The intensity of their stares meant this was no mere pep rally.

What the hell? Now I'm gonna have to pass a snake god every day on my way to and from school. What about my rights as an atheist not to be harassed by religious symbols? I worked long and hard as an Anti-Religions Legal Union volunteer to get rid of that Christmas scene. This damn thing is a hundred times worse, sitting high up on a pedestal, head poised to strike. Who dreamed up this monstrosity? I think I'll come back tonight when nobody's around and egg the stupid thing.

Something knocked Joe to his knees. Barely able to breathe, his stomach lurched, gushing his breakfast. People scattered.

Just as he was about to pass out, somebody spoke directly into his ear.

"Joseph. What did you do?"

Joe couldn't answer.

Two palms grasped his head, and foreign words were muttered. "There, that'll fix you. C'mon I'll help you up."

Joe rose and faced his helper. "Professor Stone?"

The professor was resplendent in a brilliantly plumed costume as old as The Americas.

"I asked what you did, Joseph."

"I cursed that thing."

"Haven't you learned anything in my class about respecting religious beliefs? That's not a thing. It's our sacred God. How can you expect to curse God and get away with it?"

"I don't believe in God. I told you that in class."

"Yes, and I ignored it, knowing one day you'd change your mind."

"I haven't changed my mind." An excruciating pain slammed Joe's stomach, and he fell to his knees.

"Joseph, you are the sharpest student in my class. But you're also the most closed-minded and least pragmatic. If you persist with this nonsense, I'm going to walk away and leave you here to suffer. So, what'll it be? A long hospital stay with a painful, terminal stomach ailment nobody can treat? Or believe, make a sacrifice to appease God, and live?"

"I'll believe," Joe gasped, feeling darkness closing in.

The professor repeated the healing ritual. "Indeed you will," he said, helping Joe up. "Now, take this flower, and offer it to your God. You'll see how much better you'll feel. Good things will happen. Just go and worship. It's so easy, so pleasant, so life-changing. And more thrilling than you could ever imagine."

Bewildered, Joe took the flower.

The drumming stopped. Believers sang an enchanting, seductive love song. The crowd parted, making a path for the convert.

With the professor at his side, Joe approached the coiled monstrosity. Now it glowed. Now it was an incredibly magnificent woman of gold, smiling, beckoning, spreading herself for penetration.

UNSPEAKABLE MISERY

"Welcome back to Hedonist For A Day," said the TV host after three commercials. "Every week, we select a winner from three unfortunate men who've had lives of unspeakable misery. Each contestant gets eight minutes to tell his story. Meanwhile, every member of our studio audience is fitted with tear-o-meters. As each contestant tells his tale of woe, our computer tracks the audience's tear volume. The contestant who causes the greatest outpouring of tears wins. At the end of the show, the winner is placed inside our Pleasure Palace where he'll enjoy twenty-four hours of continuous, incredible pleasure provided by fabulous women and machines. And now...let's meet our final contestant!"

A dazzling model placed a large glass jar on a table. The jar contained a severed head immersed in yellow liquid. Dozens of multi-colored wires ran from the top of the head to speakers mounted on the jar.

Removing the lid, the host spoke into the jar. "What's your name, Sir?"

"Wally," the head gurgled.

"Why do you want to be named Hedonist For A Day?"

"Isn't it obvious?"

"Sure is. But there's a devastating story here. Tell us about your unspeakable misery."

"It all started ten years ago when I was a teenager and got abducted by aliens. They took me into some kind of weird laboratory, and sliced my head off with a dull, rusty knife. But that was after they jammed hundreds of red-hot needles in the most tender parts of my body."

As the head related all the horrifying details of his abduction, thousands of home viewers fainted. Several had heart attacks. Dozens in the studio audience had to be revived by paramedics.

When Wally's time was up, the host said, "Phew! What an incredible story of tortuous suffering."

The camera switched to a large computer loaded with blinking lights. A bell sounded, and a slip of paper fell into a hopper. The host removed the slip and said, "Based on our computer's measurements of tear output, I'm pleased to announce this week's Hedonist For A Day is...Wally!"

Wally's grinning head bobbed so violently, it almost flew out of the jar.

Those in the studio audience who were still functioning applauded wildly. A studio band played a triumphant fanfare, while hundreds of balloons fell from the ceiling.

The show ended when a model carried the jar into the Pleasure Palace.

The host entered the palace and told Wally, "This is the first time a decapitated head ever won. Frankly, since you're not attached to a body, we're not sure how to apply our mind-blowing pleasure techniques. Let's try an erotic massage by three professional geishas and see what happens." Pointing to a topless pleasure provider, the host added, "Take his head out of the jar and put it on the massage table."

"No!" Wally yelled. "If you pull my wires and remove me from the fluid, I'll die within three minutes. How about putting me on the pleasure machines."

"That won't work. We'll have to immerse pleasure probes in your fluid. If we do that, you'll be electrocuted."

"Dammit! I won fair and square. You better find a way to give me the intense pleasure you promised, or I'll sue!"

The host took the show's producer aside. "This guy's a royal pain in the ass. Maybe we can say we had a computer error, and that he really didn't win."

"Good idea," the producer said. "I'll toss him a few bucks. Then we'll get him outta here."

When Wally heard the producer's offer, he screamed, "Keep your freakin' money. I want to feel every ounce of pleasure you owe me."

After the host and producer conferred again, the producer said, "Wally, we think we found an answer. We're going to put fish in your jar."

"How are fish gonna give me a good time?"

"The kind we have in mind wiggle frantically when they swim. When they brush against your face, their wiggling will give you exquisite pleasure."

"Sounds good to me," the head said.

The host dropped six fish into the jar and replaced the lid.

"Mmm," Wally gurgled. "Good choice. This is sooo nice."

Seconds later, his screams could be heard for miles.

"Look at those cute tropical fishies," squealed a pleasure provider, as she stared at the skull floating in the jar. "What kind are they?"

"Piranha," said the smiling host.

FLEA MARKET SPECIAL

"Hey, Sue, look what I got at the flea market for a buck," Harry said, putting a black metal box on the table.

"How exciting! I can't wait to see what's inside!"

Harry slammed the rusted padlock with a hammer. After a few whacks, the lock fell off.

Removing the lid, Sue screamed when she saw a woman's head.

"Take it easy," Harry said. "It ain't real. Looks like it's made from wood."

"What an ugly-looking hag. What's that button for on her forehead?"

"I don't know."

When Sue pressed the button, the head's eyes popped open. An old woman's voice cackled, and said, "Put a penny in my mouth, if you dare, and I'll tell your future."

"How neat," she said, reaching for her change purse.

"Don't do it! This thing gives me the creeps. It might be haunted. Look—it just smirked at me!"

Ignoring his pleas, Sue inserted a penny into a slot between the hag's lips. Whirring sounds filled the room. The thing's eyes rolled backward. Only the whites showed.

"You will die in five minutes," a screechy voice said.

"I told you it's haunted!" Harry yelled. "Did you hear what it just said?"

"Yeah. It's the best thing I ever heard," she said, jumping up and down. "Yeee-haw! I'm gonna win Power Ball, tonight."

"That's NOT what it said."

"I gotta buy a ticket. Power Ball's up to a hundred million. I can't believe it! I'm gonna be rich! Wa-hooo!"

Grabbing the box, Harry said, "I'm gonna burn this damn thing."

"No you're not! You might screw things up. If you ruin this for me, I swear I'll cut your heart out!"

"Listen to me. It didn't say you're gonna win anything. It said you're gonna die in just a few minutes."

"You're nuts. You're just jealous that I'm gonna win a hundred million. What are you afraid of, Harry? That I'll collect the money and run off?"

"No! I'm afraid for your life."

"Stop acting so jerky," she said, heading for the door.

Harry shoved a penny into the thing's mouth.

"You will be hung for murder," said the voice.

"Hear that?" Harry said. "Can't you see what's happening?"

"All it said was: 'you're a jerk,'" she replied. "And if I stay with you, you're gonna wreck my future."

"You evil fiend!" Harry yelled, pounding the wooden face with his hammer.

Sue tried to stop him. He shoved her aside.

"Look what you did!" she screamed. "You killed it. You rotten bastard! You ruined my future!"

She grabbed a pot and slammed Harry's head with all her might until he collapsed.

Cursing him, she tried to insert a coin between the smashed lips, but it wouldn't go into the slot. She tried to pry the lips open with a screwdriver.

"Please take my penny. Please tell me you're not mad, and that I'm still gonna win the lottery."

Suddenly, she screamed. Blood streamed from her hand.

"Why did you bite my fingers off?" she shrieked before fainting.

* * * *

The jury thought the evidence against Harry was overwhelming. He'd cut off his wife's fingers. Then her head. Since two psychiatrists affirmed his sanity, all agreed this was a case of premeditated murder.

Harry described the head in the box to detectives and how it could have maimed and murdered his wife while he was unconscious. They thought he was nuts. Especially when they searched his apartment and found nothing unusual.

Before sentencing Harry to death by hanging, the judged asked if he had anything to say.

"Yes, your Honor. I want everyone here to listen very closely. It's a matter of life or death. If you ever find a black box with a wooden head inside, don't smash its face with a hammer."

A COFFIN IS A WONDROUS THING

Randolph loved coffins. He didn't know why.

He also loved Barbie dolls. He didn't know why that was so, either.

One day, while looking at a coffin he'd bought for a buck at a garage sale, he thought, "I'll bet there's a use for a big box like this."

He tried filling it with popcorn. But somehow filling it to the brim, and adding salt and butter to the contents didn't satisfy him. He began to think the coffin was meant for something far more noble.

Next he filled the coffin with cigarette butts that had been smoked exclusively by European nobility. He found he could tuck thousands inside, but several hundred less when the butts were filter-tipped. And though he took many digital pictures of the coffin's contents from various angles, he still had the nagging feeling that the coffin wasn't fulfilling its true existential purpose.

Coffee grounds, carefully selected for their delicate aroma and collected from the city's Starbucks, were next. The coffin nicely accommodated a hundred pounds worth. And yet, after photographing the results, Randolph felt that something was still missing.

Then he thought about the bikini-clad Barbie doll that sat on the fireplace mantle. He'd always wondered what use such a thing could have, though he loved it so. It didn't work as a floor mop. It didn't improve the taste of his soup when he dipped the doll in a steaming bowl, and it didn't speed up his Internet service no matter how many times he sat the doll atop his computer monitor.

After much soul searching, his rusted frontal lobes shed their rust. Immediately, his brain filled with wondrous images. "Eureka!" he hollered.

Taking a handful of popcorn, another of unfiltered cigarette butts, and another of coffee grounds, he quickly tossed them into the coffin. Then he gently laid the doll on top of the grounds with its head pointing toward the foot of the box. After closing the lid, he spread his arms, and spun around a hundred times while singing several choruses of *Three Blind Mice*.

He got so dizzy, he passed out.

When he awoke, he found he'd shrunk. Running to a mirror, he was pleased to see that he was only eight inches tall. Though he easily climbed the coffin, he found he had to expend thousands of calories trying to open the lid.

Looking inside, he saw the Barbie doll puffing on a cigarette butt, chomping on popcorn, and lapping up coffee grounds.

"May I join you?" he asked.

"Please do," she said," as she slipped out of her bikini. "I thought you'd never ask."

"Now I know what a coffin's for," he said, as he leapt toward the giggling doll.

ICE CREAM SCOOPS

"Dammit!" Harry yelled. "I couldn't find anybody walking the streets tonight. What's a guy supposed to do to get some fresh hot chow in this town?"

"I didn't find anybody, either," Charlie said. "I spent hours combing the railroad yards. Damn place was empty. I've never been so famished."

"Screw this," Moe said. "I'm heading back to Haiti. Never missed a meal the whole time I was there. There's plenty of hot chow back there. Somebody's always getting lost in the jungle."

"Let me know when you're leaving," Charlie said. "I'll go with you."

"Hold on," Harry said. "We can always sneak into funeral homes."

"You gotta be kidding," Moe said. "There ain't no way I'd ever munch on cold, dead brains. Especially from embalmed corpses. Yuk! Ever smell the embalming fluid they put in those bodies? Let me tell you, if you ever got a whiff, you'd never even think of cracking open the heads of corpses to eat their brains. I knew a guy who was so desperate he actually ate the cold, dead brains from a guy laid out in a funeral parlor. He said he puked his calcified guts out for an hour."

"But what if we can't find anybody wandering the streets tonight? What other choice do we have?"

The three zombies fell silent, as they sat within a crypt pondering their plight.

"I got an idea," Harry said. "Before I died, I useta eat at Chinese restaurants. I useta pour lotsa soy sauce on my egg foo young. Made it extra tasty. This town has three Chinese restaurants. Why don't we go to one, get some soy sauce, take it to a funeral parlor pour it on the embalmed brains, and have dinner?"

"Need I remind you," Charlie said, "zombies ain't very popular in these parts. The minute any of us would walk into a restaurant, they'd go nuts and call the cops. You know what that means."

"Yeah," said Moe. "SWAT teams with chain saws and flame throwers."

"Maybe there's a way to get soy sauce without getting spotted," Harry said.

"Like how?"

"I'll bet lotsa customers don't eat everything on their plates. So when the dish washer gets those plates, he probably dumps the leftovers into a garbage can. When those cans are full, he probably puts them in the back alley to be picked up by a garbage truck. If we crawl inside those garbage cans and jump up and down real hard, we oughta be able to squeeze soy sauce outta the leftovers. Especially if there's lotsa chop suey in there."

"Sounds like it'll work. But what'll we put the soy sauce in so we can take it to the funeral home?"

"We can check garbage cans for empty bottles. So, let's split up, and each one of us go to a different Chinese restaurant. We'll check their garbage cans, get as much soy sauce as we can, then meet back here in an hour."

They agreed to give it a try.

An hour later, Harry, Charlie and Moe returned to the cemetery. Only one managed to get some soy sauce. Unfortunately, it was barely enough to season a spoonful of embalmed corpse brains.

"Any other brilliant ideas?" asked Moe.

"I just thought of something," Harry said. "I still have the cell phone I took from that guy I ate last week."

"So what? You don't know anybody's phone numbers. And even if you did, the way you growl when you talk, you'll scare the hell out of whoever answers."

"Suppose I call 911 and say there's a bomb hidden in the mall? That oughta scare everybody in the mall enough to make them run outside."

"Good idea," Charlie said. "The parking lot ain't lit very well. If we play our cards right, we can yank a few shoppers into the surrounding bushes. Then it'll be party time!"

"Then we all agree that I'll call 911 and say there's a bomb in the mall?" asked Harry.

Moe and Charlie nodded.

"OK. Let's head to the parking lot. Once we get to the trees surrounding the lot, I'll make the call."

Before long, they arrived at the tree-lined perimeter. All three carried ice cream scoops, the edges of which had been honed to razor sharpness.

"Get ready," Harry said. "I'm gonna call. Here goes. Hello, 911? There's a bomb in the mall." He hung up fast.

Moe tapped his scoop against a tree to mark the passing seconds. When he reached 247, shoppers poured out the mall.

"Be very quiet, and don't make a move until somebody gets real close to the trees," Charlie said.

Three shoppers moved too close to the trees.

Harry, Charlie, and Moe munched on fresh, hot brains they quickly scooped from crushed heads.

When sated, they slipped away and headed for the cemetery. Along the way, they traded tidbits about the meals they'd just enjoyed.

"Man, those were the sweetest I had in ages," Moe said. "Reminded me of candy canes."

"Mine were slightly salty—just the way I like them," Charlie said. "But now I'm thirsty."

"I sprinkled some garlic powder on mine. Dee-licious!" Harry said, picking a few gray morsels from his putrid teeth for extra chewing.

"Too bad we don't have a freezer," Moe said. "We coulda stocked up real good tonight. At least a week's worth of chow."

"Wal-Mart has lotsa freezers," Charlie said. "Maybe we can build some surplus, then find a way to hide it in their freezers. It's something to think about tomorrow. The cemetery's just ahead. Let's get a good night's sleep and work on that one with fresh minds."

"Minds?" asked Moe. "None of us has any brains left that ain't petrified by now."

"Truer words were never spoken," Harry said. "I often wonder about the irony. We don't have brains. Yet, we eat them hot and fresh every chance we get."

"Speaking of brains, I could go for a gray matter pizza with extra cheese," Charlie said. "You know—for a change of pace."

"We'll work on that tomorrow," Harry said, as they entered the moldy crypt.

THE REFUND

After the séance ended and the others had departed, Ed asked Madame Glory for a refund.

"I don't give refunds," she said. "If the spirits said something you didn't like, that's not my problem. I don't control them, they control me. However, sometimes they get out of hand. Tell you want I'll do. I'll let you attend my next séance at no charge."

"When's your next séance?"

"Next full moon."

"That's a month away!" Ed hollered. "I can't wait that long. Not after what you said."

"What did I say?"

"Don't you remember?"

"I never remember what the spirits channel through me while I'm in a trance."

"One of your spooky-sounding spirits said I'd die within 12 hours."

"I'm sorry to hear that, Sir. The spirits never lie. If they say you'll die, that's your fate. Prepare yourself for the end."

"That's just what I wanna do. I wanna die making love to a gorgeous woman. It'll cost a hundred bucks for a good-looking streetwalker. I'm almost broke. So give me a refund."

"No refunds. I cannot be held responsible for what the spirits say. You took the risk to hear the truth. You heard it. Now you want your money back. You're wasting precious time. If you have less than 12 hours to live, perhaps you should be partying right now instead of harassing me."

"I'll give you harassment!" Ed's fist knocked her backward. Her head slammed the pointy edge of a weird, demonic statue. The shock of seeing spurting blood cooled his rage.

"Dammit! She doesn't have a heart beat. Funny, but I didn't hear a spirit say she'd be dead within an hour. Maybe it was all a sham—that it was her making up things. Just to give folks the willies and make them feel like they got their money's worth. Yeah, that's what it was. Hell, I ain't gonna die. I better get out of here. But I ain't going without my refund. Hmm. Nice ring on her finger. That oughta get a few hundred at a pawn shop."

Ed didn't stop with the ring. Ransacking the apartment, he collected a fist full of jewelry and a pocket full of cash.

When he yanked open her front door to exit, he was shocked to see a huge dog blocking the way. It's red eyes and greenish glowing face froze Ed in his tracks.

"You killed my best channeler," the dog said.

"She's not dead," Ed said in a quivering voice. "She unconscious."

"I wouldn't be here if she was unconscious. As a matter of fact, she sent me to avenge her. She's waiting for you in the pit. I think you should join her. After all, you were told you'd be dead within 12 hours."

"Can't we make a deal? I'll sell you my soul for twenty more years of life? I'll be your slave. I'll do anything you say."

"Won't work. Madame Glory lied. My spirit doesn't control her. She controls me."

The beast sprang at Ed and ripped his throat.

A ROUGH CHOICE

"What a freakin' mess!" Frank yelled when confronted with walls of nearly impenetrable jungle thickets. "I thought rowing a hundred miles down the Amazon was bad, especially when the boat flipped and the crocs almost got us. This is ten times worse. How the hell are we gonna cut our way through this? For two cents, I'd forget the whole damn thing. I don't care if I go back to Chicago empty handed."

"You wanna quit after all we've gone through to get here?" Charlie asked. "Geez. You were so gung-ho about going into the Brazilian jungle to find the ruby idol."

"Hey, the stupid map made it look like a piece of cake. It just said jungle. Not hostile, demon bushes that look like something you'd expect to find in a King Kong movie. Look at that damn thing over there."

"What thing?"

"That humongous yellow flower. Look at the size of that thing. See how it's opening and closing, like it can't wait to eat us for lunch."

"Don't let your imagination go wild," Charlie said. "Remember what that old timer back in the village said about mirages from the heat when we got to the interior? That flower isn't any bigger than a lily. You better take your malaria pills."

"I took them. You're the one who needs pills. If you can't see that flower is big enough to swallow you whole, something's wrong with your freakin' eyesight."

"OK, Frank. I'll prove it to you. I'll pluck the damn thing to show you."

"Don't be stupid. If something happens to you I'll be stuck here all alone."

"What the hell's gonna happen? It's just a little flower."

When Charlie walked toward the flower, Frank saw it turn toward Charlie, as if it recognized his approach.

"Charlie! It sees you!"

Without answering, Charlie reached down to pull the flower from the soil. He heard a roar, but it was too late to avoid the yellow mass that lashed out. A second later, only his jungle boots protruded from the flower.

Frank screamed Charlie's name, as he watched the boots disappear inside the flower.

Falling to his knees in anguish, he heard a thunderous burp and saw a pair of boots flying toward him. Before he could duck, they slammed his head, knocking him unconscious.

When he woke, he saw snapping crocodiles creeping toward him. One almost grabbed his foot.

He emptied his pistol with no effect. With the jungle his only salvation, he grabbed his machete, and rushed toward it.

That's when he saw hundreds of huge yellow flowers turning his way.

SAGE ADVICE

Dear Auntie Em,

My husband thinks he's turning into a fly. What should I do?

—Distressed.

Dear Distressed,

Buy a flyswatter and a bucket of warm horse dung.

— Auntie Em. PS: No problem is so big it can't be run away from.

Dear Auntie Em,

As you suggested, I bought a flyswatter. But he's too fast for me. Should I swat him when he's rubbing his front legs together, as if he's washing his hands, which are no longer there? As to the horse dung, it cooled down too fast, so it didn't attract him. I tried to heat it, but the whole pile blew up inside the microwave. I had to buy a new microwave. Got any ideas on how to keep horse dung warm, other than using a microwave?

— Really Distressed

Dear Really Distressed,

Go to G-Mart and buy one of their new special microwaveable dung dishes, guaranteed by Ladies Good Homekeeping. Use it to heat the dung. Don't ever try to swat a fly when he's washing his hands. Flies are compulsive hand washers. If you manage to kill him during his ritual, he'll come back to haunt you. Then you'll have big-time problems. Especially since nobody knows how to kill ghost flies.

— Auntie Em. PS: No problem is so big it can't be run away from.

Dear Auntie Em,

You told me to buy a dung dish at G-Mart. I did. It cost $79.95 plus tax. But it does the job. Now I can warm up horse dung and place it around the house. Yesterday, I saw my husband, who turned into a fly, lighting on a soft steaming pile. I slammed it hard. Missed him. Now I gotta repaint the walls. Plus, I got infected, brown zits Do you think I should get some fly-eating spiders?

— Really Super Distressed

Dear Really Super Distressed,

Get the Martha Stewgut brand of fly-eating spiders. They're guaranteed by Ladies Good Homekeeping. And they are environmentally friendly. Meanwhile, get rid of the flyswatter and whatever dung didn't stick to your walls and face—that's old technology.

— Auntie Em. PS: No problem is so big it can't be run away from.

Dear Auntie Em,

I got the Martha Stewgut fly-eating spiders you recommended. Now the house is full of spider webs. My pet canary got loose and got caught in one. The spiders tore him apart and ate him. I miss my birdie very much. Do you think he gave his life for a good cause, and I should arrange for an open coffin showing in the State Capitol Rotunda?

Meanwhile, my husband got caught in one of their nets. But they ate so much bird, they're too full to attack and eat him. What can I do to increase their appetites? I tried to tell them my husband, the fly, was caught in their biggest net. But they don't understand English.

— Super Distressed To The Nth Degree

Dear Super Distressed To The Nth Degree,

Go to G-Mart and buy their brand chocolate syrup. Coat your husband with two tablespoons. Spiders like chocolate. Coat yourself too —-if you have a spider fetish, like the one mentioned in the latest Good Homekeeping article, "50 Ways to Make It Even Better."

— Auntie Em. PS: No problem is so big it can't be run away from.

Dear Auntie Em,

Thank you for all your wonderful advice. The article was an eye opener. The thing with the chocolate was inspired. I'm a new woman. And I'm now a widow. But not for long.

Do you believe in polygamy? With spiders?

— Sticky But Thrilled.

TRANSFORMATIONS

Another hard day slaving over the Petrie dish. Though I'd spent eighteen grueling hours injecting 783 different liquid compounds into the gooey, greenish-white clump of mashed potatoes, it refused to transform into a dinosaur embryo. It just sat there doing nothing, as if mocking me. Enraged, I wanted to destroy the unresponsive mass.

"You dirty sonovabitch! What the hell do you need? I've given you $15,735 worth of the purest compounds in existence. Why don't you respond?"

Something my sainted mother used to say popped into my mind, "Spaghetti is the staff of life. When all fails, have some spaghetti."

Racing to the kitchen, I grabbed three spaghetti strands—remnants of yesterday's dinner—and pressed them into the moldy mashed potatoes. I left one trailing outside like a fuse. Lighting it with the Bunsen burner, I ran for cover and hid under my bombproof desk.

Nothing happened. Dammit! I'd obviously done something wrong. But what? Perhaps I should've inserted a fourth strand.

Then it dawned on me. Maybe Mom had been speaking cryptically. Could she have meant something deeply metaphysical?

I pondered the possibility while repeating her words. Then I realized spaghetti includes sauce, or it isn't bona fide, orthodox spaghetti. Marinara sauce has near-magical properties and makes eating pasta a transcending experience.

"Sauce is the lifeblood of spaghetti," I reasoned. "That's why it's so red. Lifeblood...lifeblood...lifeblood."

Plunging a syringe into the marinara, I drew 100cc. I must've broken Olympic records as I raced back to the Petrie dish. Slamming the syringe into the lump of mashed potatoes, I pressed my thumb hard against the plunger. When the syringe was empty, I counted. By the time I reached 39, the mass emitted a sound like the sigh of a contented lover. Eureka!

"Thanks, Mom for your exquisite wisdom of the ages," I muttered.

* * * *

Four hours after injecting spaghetti sauce, the mass started to grow by one millimeter every 13.293 minutes.

* * * *

I didn't sleep for three days. I couldn't. Not after making the most amazing discovery in the universe. Miraculously, the original cup of moldy mashed potatoes transmogrified into another substance: ravioli.

By midnight, the ravioli had further transmogrified into triple-layered lasagna. My scientific intuition urged me to act immediately. Running to the kitchen, I drew another 100cc of marinara sauce, and injected it into the lasagna. Once again, the substance sighed. Then it emitted a second sound that sounded like a greeting in Italian.

I pressed my stethoscope against the lasagna. My Lord! A regular heartbeat! Jumping up and down, I yelled in triumph. I'd just created the world's first living lasagna!

Soon, lack of sleep and fatigue struck with a vengeance. Before collapsing, I put the Petrie dish and its precious contents into the freezer to retard further transmogrification.

Within minutes, I was sound asleep.

Eighteen hours later, I woke feeling refreshed. As my mind cleared, I remembered I'd created one of the wonders of the world. Yanking open the freezer door to gaze upon my fabulous creation, I found it covered with three inches of frost. Worse, I couldn't find a heartbeat.

Chiseling an opening through the frost and noodle topping, I gave the lasagna mouth-to-mouth.

No response.

Frantic, I threw the lasagna into the microwave. Sixty-five seconds later, I checked again. Still nothing.

Placing my creation on the lab table, I yelled, "Clear!" and pressed paddles against the lasagna. Though a million volts surged through the lasagna, it didn't stir.

My mother's advice came to mind again. I raced to the kitchen, grabbed the saucepot and dumped the entire contents over the lasagna. After what seemed forever, it sighed and said something in Italian.

The lasagna didn't transform into a dinosaur embryo, as I'd calculated. Instead, it sprouted long strands of black hair on one end. Then feet and shapely legs on the other. This was followed by buttocks and abdomen. On and on it went, until it turned into a magnificent woman.

Unfortunately, she was only large enough to fit in the Petrie dish.

Instead of being glad she was alive, she started bitching in Italian about her miniscule stature. She never stopped nagging.

To shut her up, I put her in the freezer. By the time I removed her, she was forever silenced.

Next time I conduct this experiment, I'll use a hundred pounds of moldy mashed potatoes and ten gallons of marinara.

JAKE'S NEW MEDICINE

"Where have you been for two days?" Ruth hollered. "Everybody's been going crazy looking for you!"

"Don't holler at me," Jake said. "I was doing what you've been nagging me about for the past year."

"Whadda ya mean?"

"I was saving whales like you and your West End Environmental Club are always harping about. Only instead of just talking about it like you do, I actually did something."

"You were saving whales for the past two days?"

"Yes."

"What a liar! Such a shame an eighty-five year old rabbi has to start lying."

"It's the truth. Just hear me out. I have proof. This letter. It's still a bit wet. Let's dry it out, then you'll be able to read better what it says."

"So why do I have to wait until it's dry? Why don't you tell me what it says?"

"OK. It's a letter of commendation. From the whales. For saving them. Even more important, the last paragraph names me their President for life. They had a big meeting last night, and held the first election in their history. I won."

"That's enough, already. I'm calling Dr. Saperstein. That new medicine he gave you is doing funny things to your brain. He said there was a small chance that might happen."

"Listen to me, Ruth, before you start calling doctors. While you were helping your sister with the dishes on Thanksgiving, I told you I was going for a walk. Remember?"

"Yeah. And that's the last I saw you until now."

"Well, I went for a walk along the beach. And then something remarkable happened. I know you're going to find this hard to believe, but a pink whale beached just a hundred feet ahead of me. So, I ran toward it. As I approached, it opened one eye, looked at me, and said, 'Please save us, Mister.'"

"A whale talked to you? Now I know you've been hallucinating."

"I'm telling the truth. This was no hallucination."

"OK, so let's say it asked you for help. What kind of help? To push it back into the ocean?"

"No. When I asked it what kind of help the whales needed, it said, 'We're sick of eating fish. We want caramel covered popcorn.' So, I went to Wal-Mart, bought a few boxes of caramel covered popcorn, opened the whale's mouth and poured in a whole box. You should have seen how happy he was. Ever hear a whale laugh? It's a marvelous thing to behold."

"That's it! I'm calling Dr. Saperstein right now!"

"If I were you, I wouldn't waste time calling doctors. I'd spend the time thinking about what I was going to wear for the Inaugural Ball. It's tomorrow, after the swearing in ceremony. You don't have much time to get ready. And since you're going to be the First Lady of the first President of the whales, I think it's important you make a good impression. Plus, we got to start calling people. I want everybody we know to be there."

Ruth grabbed her cell phone and called Saperstein. While they were buzzing, Jake jotted ideas down for his inaugural speech.

"The doctor wants to see you right now. Take a quick shower while I move the car from the garage."

The moment she left, Jake used his cell phone. "Hello, Harry?" This is Jake. Yes, your new President-elect. Look, things aren't turning out the way I hoped. My wife doesn't believe me. I'll have to run my administration without her. Meanwhile, have you come up with any ideas for which of your fellow whales might make a good Secretary of Defense? Oh...that's great. He sounds perfect."

When Ruth came back into the house to get Jake, he was nowhere to be found.

That night, a CNN newscaster told of a curious sighting off the coast of California. "A man scanning the beach with a metal detector said he saw a senior citizen walking on the sand. Suddenly, a pink whale leaped out of the water and slid up the beach right in front of the senior. It opened its mouth and the old guy walked inside. The whale slid back into the ocean and disappeared. The beachcomber swears the pink whale was wearing a red, white, and blue hat that said, Don't Make a Mistake. Vote for Jake."

All the commentators chuckled. One of them made a light-hearted comment about drunks seeing pink whales instead of pink elephants.

HIGH FEVER

When torrential rains came, my house flooded. Suffering from flu and high fever, there was little I could do to escape.

One minute I was looking at the downpour through my bedroom window, and the next I was knocked off my feet by rampaging floodwaters. Everything went topsy-turvy. I thought I was gonna drown.

Suddenly, arms grabbed me. I musta passed out.

When I woke, a craggy, greenish face was close enough to kiss. Eyes stared deeply into mine, as if searching for answers to life's most ponderous enigmas. I wanted to scream, but didn't have the energy.

I remember thinking, Orange eyes. Who the hell has three orange eyes?

As I trembled violently, the eyes' owner climbed on top of me. Warmth coursed throughout my body. Then my rescuer began to chirp. The melodic sounds calmed me and made me feel strong again. And then stronger. And even stronger yet, as if I could conquer the universe.

That's when I felt ecstatic surges through every muscle, every nerve. I found myself crying out for mercy, yet wanting more. Overwhelmed by the intensity, I passed out.

"You're gonna be OK," said a nurse. She was standing in a rowboat. Water was just inches below my bed's mattress.

"How'd I get here?" I asked, remembering my encounter with three orange eyes, and wondering if I'd hallucinated.

"If I told you, you wouldn't believe me," the nurse said. "In fact, some guys from Homeland Security have been waiting for you to regain consciousness. Do you feel strong enough to talk to them?"

"Why Homeland Security?"

"It has to do with how you got to this hospital. And everything that's happened since flash floods hit us two days ago. I was here when she brought you in. You better brace yourself. When the waters recede, and word gets out, this place is gonna be crawling with reporters. You'll probably make millions outta this."

"I still don't know what you're talking about."

She gave a cynical look. "Didn't anybody ever tell you about abstinence? Especially when it comes to strange stuff?"

"Dammit! Tell me what the hell's going on!"

"So you're gonna play innocent to the bitter end. OK, have it your way. I'm gonna row to the next wing. I'll be back in five minutes. Oh, by the way, she's also a patient here."

When the nurse rowed away, my thoughts drifted back to the green face, orange eyes, melodious chirping, the weight of something pressing against me, and the electrifying sensations that had jolted me to the marrow. Then I realized whoever owned those eyes had saved me. I owed her. Freak-eyed or no, I owed her.

Minutes later, the nurse returned in her rowboat. A basin, covered with a cloth was on the seat. Extending it toward me, she said, "This is for you. It's from her."

When I removed the cloth, hundreds of orange-eyed things chirped frantically.

THE VEIL

A few hours before Geoffrey Winston was to assassinate a key German agent in Lisbon, he was summoned to his Director's office.

"I want you to drop everything and deliver this package to Serge Sosa in Casablanca," the Director said. "Your plane leaves in four hours."

"What about tonight's mission? The target's heading back to Germany tomorrow. Everything's in place. I may never get another opportunity to eliminate the bastard."

"The mission's canceled. I'm afraid the Prime Minister's Office has decided this is more important. What's more, he selected you to deliver the package."

"Why does he want me to play messenger boy for that bloody bandit?"

"Sosa told the PM he'd accept the package only from your hands."

"What's in the bloody thing?"

"I wasn't informed. Whatever it is, it's quite light. But no doubt, extremely valuable. Look, I understand your frustration. Sometimes I think the Prime Minister has his head up his arse. Here's a German passport in the name of Adolf Zilker. You're now a salesman from a Berlin company that manufactures gambling equipment. A false-bottomed suitcase has already been packed with the usual things. It's in the secretary's office. Oh by the way, no weapons this trip. Not even a knife. Is that clear?"

"Yes, General."

Cursing the Prime Minister, Serge Sosa, and the entire British Intelligence Establishment, Winston got the suitcase and caught a cab to the Lisbon Aerodrome.

After a flight in a Ford Tri-Motor Aeroplane, Winston cleared customs at Casablanca and headed for Sosa's Café Chicago. The name was just a gimmick to attract customers. In the 1930s, anything American was considered exotic in North Africa, especially if it was connected with Chicago.

Serge Sosa, an informant for British Intelligence had never been to America. Nobody was even sure if Sosa was his real last name. He was one of millions of displaced persons who'd lost their documents during World War One. Migrating to French Morocco in 1920, he'd built a sizable fortune, though he was a Communist. Some reports in his dossier implied his money was supplied by Lenin's secret police, and that he was one of their high-level operatives. Winston had some dealings with Sosa before and didn't trust the man.

Entering Café Chicago, he was struck by the electric atmosphere. A band played American jazz better than he'd ever heard outside England. The air was abuzz with the babble of a dozen languages. A mixture of nationalities, mainly Europeans, filled the tables.

The maitre d' asked Winston if he wished to dine. Speaking in German-accented English, he declined, announcing he was Adolf Zilker from Berlin and had an appointment with the café's owner. Winston flashed a German business card emblazoned with a swastika.

The sight of that Nazi symbol excited the maitre d', a fascist sympathizer. "Certainly, Herr Zilker," he said crisply. "Monsieur Sosa is expecting you." He clapped his hands, and a mean-looking Spaniard in a vanilla suit appeared. "Carlos, take Herr Zilker to Sosa's office. He's expected."

Winston noticed a bulge on the right side of Carlos' suit jacket. He wished he too had the comfort of a holstered pistol. But now he knew where he could get one, in case things got a bit sticky.

After climbing a spiral staircase, Carlos knocked on an intricately carved door. A huge African brandishing a Thompson submachine gun opened the door part way.

"He's expected," Carlos said.

The African opened the door wide enough for Winston and Carlos to enter.

Serge Sosa greeted Winston with a vigorous handshake. "Herr Zilker, how are you? How are your lovely wife and children? How was the flight from Berlin?"

While Winston answered his questions, Sosa dismissed Carlos and the African. As soon as they were gone, he said, "Good to see you again, Winston. I heard you're creating quite a stir among the Germans in Lisbon."

"I do what I can," Winston said dryly.

"Don't be so modest. Your work has put quite a dent in their operations. I hear they just put a price on your head."

Alarmed at the news, Winston maintained a poker face. He wondered if it were true. He made a mental note to check his sources throughout Europe as soon as he returned to Lisbon. Then it dawned on him that might not make it back. Maybe Sosa would deliver him to the Germans for a fat fee. Winston scanned the room to see if there were any windows from which he could make a hasty escape. Unfortunately there were none.

"I assume you have my package?"

"It's right here." Winston reached inside the suitcase and pressed a hidden latch. The door to the secret compartment popped open. He removed the small package and gave it to Sosa.

Sosa's eyes gleamed manically. "This is my ticket out of this rotten, god-forsaken, African stink hole." He pressed the package against his chest as if embracing it.

"I should be getting along. It was a tiring flight."

"I'd prefer that you stay and enjoy some refreshments. At a time like this, I'd like the company of someone to share this tremendous moment. Someone refined and cultured who can appreciate what I'm about to open."

"I don't know if I'm as refined and cultured as you imagine."

"Indeed you are. You're far more cultured than the brigands in my employ. Oh, I know plenty about you, Winston. You're tough as nails. Dangerous. Deadly. Nothing stands in your way when you're on a mission. Nevertheless, you are a refined man. Oxford educated. You love opera and ballet. You paint wonderfully detailed landscapes. You wrote a book of poems that was published under your real name—James S. Foxworthy."

"Foxworthy? Poet?" Winston forced a laugh. "That's rich, Sosa. Unfortunately, your information is quite flawed. I couldn't draw if my life depended on it. And I loathe opera and ballet."

"I could turn you over to the Germans right now, you know?"

Winston stopped laughing. "I suppose you could."

"But I won't. You are exceedingly valuable to me. I have great plans for you. In fact, James S. Foxworthy, AKA Geoffrey Winston, you're here because I demanded that London send you. I told your Prime Minister that you were the only person I trusted to deliver this package. They damn well owed me. Do you know that because of me, not a single undercover German agent who ever put his foot on African soil from Cairo to Casablanca has lived to talk about it?"

"Where do you get off making such a claim? The King of Morocco's security forces handle the Germans for us in North Africa. We arm his people and pay him in gold."

"Let's just say His Highness subcontracted the task to me," Sosa said. "Secretly, of course. You English think you know everything."

"I suspect you've been paid quite handsomely by the King."

"Not nearly enough!"

"I'd have thought the King would pay a sultan's ransom. He's no lover of the Germans. He can lose his country if they war on the French and occupy Morocco. Bad enough the French run the country, where he's just the titular leader. But things will be worse if the Germans grab Morocco. The King and his entire tribe will be annihilated. Your life won't be worth a sou, either. Hitler hates Communists as much as he hates Jews."

"No matter. The English owed me for delivering the head of German intelligence operations in Algeria to them. I told London I didn't want money or gold for my services. I wanted something far more valuable. And here it is. Aren't you curious about what's inside this package?"

"Not particularly," Winston lied.

"You'll feel differently when I open it."

Sosa quickly unwrapped the package and removed a silvery-blue, shimmering cloth the size of a towel. His heart quickened as he unfolded it. "Look how beautiful it is," he said ecstatically.

Putting the cloth to his face, he rubbed it against his cheeks. He sniffed deeply as if it were the perfumed undergarments of an exotic paramour. "I smell power!" he roared.

Winston wondered if the man were daft. He thought Sosa was having a psychotic breakdown over a piece of cloth.

"This is worth more to me than all the gold in the Bank of England. This magnificent cloth is the veil of Scheherazade, exotic princess of the desert. Daughter of the Great Sultan of Arabia. Creator of the Tales of Arabian Nights."

"Scheherazade? She's nothing more than a character in Arabic fiction. A figment of somebody's imagination."

"An old papyrus says otherwise. It tells of a day when Allah strolled through his gardens pondering what to create to reflect his glory. The accursed Serpent appeared and hissed, 'Can Allah, the Compassionate, make from the rib of man, a woman more beautiful than Eve? A woman so beautiful that Allah himself would not dare gaze into her countenance?' Allah dismissed the serpent shouting 'Thou shalt not tempt the Almighty One, the Giver and Taker of Life.' Not long afterward, the Creator of All Things Visible and Invisible put Adam into a deep slumber and breathed on his rib a second time. Thus, he formed a woman more beautiful than Eve."

"And that woman was Scheherazade?" Winston asked, amused by the Arabic fable.

"None other."

"So you're convinced this cloth is her veil?"

"The one and only. The papyrus tells how it was woven by cherubs in the Garden of Unending Delights. It was taken to Scheherazade by

Angel Gabriel. He placed the veil over her head during evening prayers to protect her beauty from the corrupt eyes of sinful men. A genie was implanted into each off its thousand and one strands. Hence the veil is possessed by a thousand and one genies. Each has the power to grant three wishes to the veil's owner."

"Three wishes for every genie?" Winston chuckled. "What happens when a bloody genie grants all three?"

"It's released to the Vale of Everlasting Tranquility, and the strand turns to brass. As you can see, none of the strands are brass. Therefore, not a single genie has ever been invoked to grant wishes. Do you understand the significance of this tremendous truth?"

Winston shrugged. He couldn't comprehend how Sosa could survive World War One, build a fortune, outwit the Germans—all very real events—and believe in fables.

"You believe in nothing," Sosa said with disgust. Wagging his finger he added, "Very soon you will learn to believe in all things. This veil, this treasure from the glorious past of wandering desert tribes, still has three thousand and three wishes to grant. And now I own it." His eyes gleamed as he laughed triumphantly.

"Let me guess," Winston said. "You'll use the wishes to rule the world."

"Indeed! I will own the world and all it contains. I will be the richest and most powerful man in history. My kingdom will be more glorious than the Inca and Aztec empires, more vast than the Romans or Alexander the Great ever dreamed of."

The way Sosa spoke made Winston think that Hitler, Mussolini, and Japan's Emperor were more preferable adversaries. They merely hoped to carve up the world into colonies and impose their governments and cultures. Adequate armed forces were available to ensure their wishes would never be realized. But, if Sosa's claims were even remotely possible, he could become the greatest menace ever. All the combined armies of the Earth couldn't stop him. Winston cringed at the idea of Serge Sosa becoming ruler of the entire globe.

"Why not become the world's greatest hero by invoking a genie and asking for world peace?" Winston asked.

"Surely you jest. Peace does not exist, except in the minds of weaklings. These are genies, not gods."

"Then what good is a genie? Or a thousand?"

"Genies fetch things for the veil's owner. Things that already exist. So, I must be very clever and plan exactly what I want them to gather. I can, for example, ask for all the diamonds in the world. The papyrus says the genies must comply. In minutes, they will collect every diamond on Earth. From rings, necklaces, bank vaults, South African mines."

"They sound like bloody thieves to me," Winston said.

"They are no worse than Robin Hood, a thief your nation elevated to near-sainthood. Surely you, an Englishman, can appreciate what three thousand Robin Hoods could accomplish."

"So, you intend to steal from the rich and give to the poor?"

"Give to the poor? Ridiculous! Who can build an empire by squandering money on masses of unwashed peasants? My plans for the poor—in fact for everyone—are far more elegant. I'll command a genie to gather the frontal lobes of every human being on the planet, except for myself and a few assistants. Billions of mindless robots robbed of their ability to think will follow my orders without question. Imagine...all that power from a single wish. And three thousand and two wishes would still remain. Can you comprehend the limitless power that lies at my fingertips?"

If there were any truth to Sosa's mind-boggling claims, Winston would have to act quickly before he lost his frontal lobes. He trembled at the thought of becoming a human robot in service to a madman.

"Are you sure the bloody thing works?" Winston asked. "Maybe you should make a wish to test the genies. Perhaps they are asleep and must be awakened. Or maybe they've lost their powers over the centuries."

Sosa blanched. The thought of a powerless veil had never occurred to him. "It is said that he who strokes the strands in faith is rewarded with beautiful, celestial music. The very music to which the planets dance as they rotate around the Sun."

Draping the veil over his arm, Sosa stroked the strands. The room filled with exquisite, ethereal sounds that made Winston think of angelic voices. Lasting only a few seconds, the sounds were the most enthralling they'd ever heard.

"So, it made some nice music. Making a bit of music isn't the same as invoking a genie and commanding it to fulfill a wish. Why not summon a genie and ask it to supply you with a thousand each of the largest and finest African diamonds, Burmese rubies, Columbian emeralds, and Ceylonese sapphires?"

Sosa reached for a crystal cognac snifter and poured golden liquid from a decanter. Taking a sip, he said, "Your idea about jewels is inspired. I may spare your frontal lobes when I build my empire. A servant who can think creatively might be of value." Grasping the first strand between his thumb and middle finger, he said, "Genie of the first strand, I invoke thee."

A gust of wind whipped through the room. Everything made of glass jingled.

"Genie of the first strand, I command thee to bring me in crystal urns, a thousand each of the largest and finest African diamonds, Burmese rubies, Colombian emeralds, and Ceylonese sapphires."

An unearthly voice said, "Yes, Master."

A fog formed in one corner of the room. A flash of lightening cracked through the mist. The fog parted revealing four crystal urns filled with magnificent stones. The highly polished gems threw flashes of colored light everywhere.

"How exquisite!" Sosa gasped. "This is truly a vision of Paradise."

Winston trembled. No man should have such power. Something had to be done quickly to stop Sosa. He thought of the cyanide pill, his constant companion since he'd entered clandestine service.

"Look how wonderfully these diamonds sparkle!" Sosa said with excitement, as he ran his hands through the stones. Moving to the rubies, he dug into them with both hands. "Look how they catch the light! What fire!"

As Sosa moved to the emeralds, Winston quickly removed a steel capsule from his pocket. Opening it, he dumped a tiny cyanide pill into Sosa's cognac snifter.

"These gems must be worth billions," Winston said.

"It's not enough! I want more! I want it all! Now there's nothing to stop me from getting it all!"

"Then let us drink to your new Empire," Winston shouted, trying to emulate Sosa's crazed enthusiasm. "Let's toast a new golden age. A new world order."

"Ah, has the unflappable Geoffrey Winston come to his senses? Is he really beginning to see the light and where his future truly lies?"

"Indeed!" Winston said.

"Well then, let us also toast the end of your servility to the Crown of England, and to the glories of your new life as servant to Serge Sosa, Emperor of the Earth."

"It's clear that the future of the world is in your capable hands," Winston said, cursing Sosa under his breath.

Pleased with Winston's response, Sosa poured him cognac, and added more to his own glass.

The agent of death had completely dissolved. One gulp was all that stood between Sosa the powerful madman and Sosa the powerless corpse. It'd only take thirty seconds to hurl him into the clutches of eternity.

"Today I drink the finest cognac. Tomorrow, I'll drink the nectar of the gods as one of their equals."

"Hear, hear!" Winston shouted, raising his glass.

Sosa swallowed his drink and poured another.

"What's your next wish?" Winston asked, counting the seconds.

Sosa gagged, his eyes wide with shock. "You bast—!" He reached for the veil in a desperate attempt to save himself.

His hands shook violently, as he tried to grasp a strand. The veil slipped from his fingers when he collapsed.

Winston pressed his fingers against Sosa's neck. No pulse. He put his ear against Sosa's chest. No heartbeat. "Burn in hell, you bloody bastard!" he yelled, kicking the corpse in the ribs with all his might.

Scooping several handfuls from each urn, Winston threw the jewels into his suitcase. He picked up the veil, grabbed the first string, and imitated the genie-invoking ritual.

"Genie of the first strand, return the jewels in the crystal urns where you found them,"

"Yes, Master."

When the gems disappeared, he ordered the genie to whisk him and his suitcase back to his Lisbon apartment. In the blink of an eye, he found himself in his living room. Throwing the veil over a chair, he poured a whiskey. While drinking, he pondered the evening's bizarre events. They seemed unbelievable, impossible, unreal. But that changed when he glanced at the veil and noticed the first strand had changed to brass.

Winston realized that he was now the owner of the shimmering cloth infested with genies. Realizing he was most powerful man on the planet, a war erupted in his soul: a profound struggle between altruism and self-interest. On one hand he could alter the course of history for the good of mankind. He could order genies to transport Germany's Hitler to the most impenetrable jungle in the Amazon, Italy's Mussolini to the middle of Antarctica, and Japan's Emperor to the top of Mount Everest.

On the other hand, why waste valuable wishes for the benefit of mankind, when he could use them to build a fabulous life for himself? What did mankind ever do for him? So what if war came? He'd order the genies to transport him to a place of safety and serenity, a place where he'd be oblivious to the coming cataclysm.

Self-interest got the upper hand. Two days passed without sleep as Winston feverishly wrote endless lists to plan his future. He structured a utopia, a carefully planned Garden of Eden. He'd live on the most beautiful Pacific island on Earth. He'd outfit it with a lifetime of the world's finest provisions, including French Champagne, American cigarettes, Belgian chocolates, English stout. He'd appropriate the most beautiful mansion in the world, and fill it with the world's greatest books. He'd staff the mansion with dozens of Europe's most gracious servants. He'd relocate to his island a hundred of the world's wittiest, friendliest, and most brilliant English-speaking intellectuals. He'd stock his bedroom with a thousand of the loveliest, most ardent women on Earth.

When he completed his list, Winston decided he'd outdone the Creator of the Cosmos by ensuring no serpents would inhabit the new Eden. By then, he was convinced that he too was a god, the supreme ruler of his own universe.

Physically, mentally, and emotionally drained, he fell asleep. His slumber was disturbed by horrible dreams. He witnessed Sosa burning in Hell, tormented by demons. He found himself struggling mightily against endless legions of German agents. He saw Angel Gabriel standing on top of Mount Ararat, blowing a golden trumpet. The blare unleashed countless genies who descended on Winston's Eden, destroying it with fire and brimstone. Winston fled in terror. When he turned to look back at the horrible destruction, he was transformed into a pillar of salt.

The nightmare hurled him from bed. Panicked, he ran to a mirror to see if he was covered with salt.

When calm returned, he realized he'd become as mad as Serge Sosa. Like Sosa, he had been corrupted by the powers that bewitched the veil. He realized the veil was more dangerous to civilization than all of its combined enemies. No wonder Scheherazade never made a wish. She must have known how dangerous the veil's power truly was.

Nothing with such potential for evil could have possibly been woven by holy angels, he reasoned. It must have emerged from the depths of Gehenna. It must have been conceived by the Serpent, whose minions wove the threads while shrieking blasphemies upon each strand.

Something had to be done about this insidious manifestation of evil. Once again it fell upon Winston to save the world. But this time, cyanide pills were useless. So were all the weapons ever devised. He was dealing with the powers of darkness, an invisible world that could never be destroyed by mankind. But if he couldn't destroy that intangible world, perhaps he could hinder it from polluting mankind's affairs.

A plan formed in his mind. He wondered if the entities within the veil could hinder the plan's execution. Genies could be devilishly clever. He'd have to articulate his wish very carefully. He wondered if the genie, upon hearing the wish, would refuse to comply. Didn't the papyrus, according to Sosa, indicate they always granted wishes? But the papyrus could have been a devious document of half-truths and lies. Or it might have contained some truths merely to advance great untruths.

Grasping the second strand with his thumb and middle finger, he invoked a genie. "Genie of the second strand, bury this veil one hundred miles below the surface of the most inaccessible place in the Sahara Desert."

"Yes, Master."

The veil disappeared in a puff of acrid smoke. The pungent odor of sulfur remained in Winston's apartment for several hours as a stark testimony of the veil's true origin.

* * * *

War came to Europe in September, 1939. During the darkest day of that horrendous six-year conflict, Winston sometimes wished he had the veil so he could dispatch Hitler to an impenetrable jungle, Mussolini to the middle of Antartica, and the Emperor of Japan to the top of Mount Everest. But then he'd recall how the veil's owner could be transformed into a monster worse than jack-booted brown shirts and banzai-charging fanatics. He'd also remember the nightmare in which he'd been turned into a pillar of salt.

* * * *

After the war, Winston traveled to cities where gemstones were sold for exorbitant prices. The proceeds from the diamonds, rubies, emeralds, and sapphires he'd appropriated that night at Sosa's enabled him to create a lesser, but exceptionally luxurious version of the Eden he'd once so carefully planned.

A NATIONAL EMERGENCY

"How did you get this wound in your arm, Detective Brown?" asked the doctor.

"I was chasing hoods on the docks," I said. "A guy came at me outta nowhere with a machete. Nicked me on the arm before I plugged him in the head."

"Lie down. This is gonna sting."

My cell phone rang.

"Hey, Brownie. Smiley here. Heard you got cut. Bad?"

"Nah. Just needs some stitches."

"Your stiff's right in front of me," Smiley said. "I started the autopsy. You sitting down?"

"Laying down. What's up?"

"Something's very strange. The back of his head shoulda been blown off. But it ain't. There's no blood anywhere. Stuck my finger in the hole you blew in his forehead. Instead of brain tissue, I felt something weird. I looked inside with a light. I don't know how to say this."

"Say what?"

"The guy doesn't have any brains. Something else is there."

"What?" I asked.

"Looks like duct tape."

I hung up. Smiley jokes a lot. But I wasn't in the mood for a Saturday night comedy routine.

My phone rang again.

"I ain't lying," Smiley said. "There's no brains in the guy's head. Just wads of duct tape. I'm about to open his chest. I'll let you know what I find."

"I ain't laughing, Smiley. So, cut the crap already." I hung up on him again.

When the doc said, "All finished," Smiley called a third time.

"I swear on my mother's eyes," Smiley said. "I've seen weird stuff in my life, but nothing like this. He doesn't have a heart. The only thing there is a plastic box. I opened it up. It was filled with wads of duct tape."

"Did you tell Homeland Security?"

"Yeah. They snickered and hung up. Would you ask your FBI buddy to come over and take a look so he can verify this?"

I figured if Smiley was willing to go so far, something was definitely wrong.

"I'll call him right now," I said. "See you at the morgue in twenty minutes."

* * * *

"What do you think, Smiley?" I asked, tapping the duct tape inside the cadaver's open skull with my pistol.

"I ain't sure. How do you explain a guy who's walking around with no blood in his body and duct tape for a brain? And more duct tape where his heart should be?"

"Maybe he's an alien," I said.

"Could be. Actually, he ain't a he. There's nothing down there except a big hole. I ran my hands inside."

"What did you find?"

"More duct tape."

"Damn! Bad enough we got terrorists, illegal aliens, gangs, overpriced gasoline, war. Now we got a Duct Tape Monster. At least I know how to kill them, if any more show up."

The doors swung open revealing Dave, my FBI contact.

"Hey, Davey," I called. "How's it going?"

Instead of answering, he opened his coat, pulled out a machete, and swung it at Smiley's neck. I pulled my pistol and shot Dave in the head.

If Smiley hadn't ducked, his head would've been on the other side of the room.

"Quick!" I yelled. "Check the wound!"

"There's no blood," Smiley said, pulling a wad of silver-colored duct tape from Dave's head.

Aghast, I dialed the police panic number.

In minutes, the morgue was a madhouse. The mayor and her staff, a Homeland Security team, and police brass ran in circles, yelling on cell phones.

"What do you think, Smiley?" asked the Police Commissioner.

"We got a helluva problem on our hands," Smiley replied. "We don't know who's infected, why, or how it happens."

"But we know how to kill them." I said.

Somebody screamed. The Police Chief's severed head whizzed past my right shoulder.

"Lookout, Brown!" somebody hollered.

I twisted just in time to see Her Honor, the Mayor, charging at me with a blood-soaked machete. I shot her right between the eyes.

"She pulled it out of her briefcase," the Commissioner yelled. "Search every briefcase in the room! Round up everybody who has a machete! Post armed guards wherever they sell them!"

"Search all incoming ships and aircraft!" said a Homeland Security agent into a phone. "Tell citizens to be on the lookout and report anybody who's carrying a machete."

"There may be thousands of them," somebody shouted. "How in the hell are we gonna identify them?"

"We'll have to X-ray the heads of everybody in the nation," Smiley said. "It's gonna be a logistical nightmare. We'll have to do it at thousands of places. Combat-ready troops will have to stand guard at every X-ray machine. The moment a monster is identified, they'll have to shoot the damn thing right on the spot."

"Problem is," a police captain said, "the guy next door might already be one. Maybe a sweet grandma is about to hack off a little kid's head. No doubt day care providers are infected. Same with our moms, religious leaders, congressmen."

"And our wives," I mumbled, checking my ammunition supply.

The room grew silent as everyone pondered the horrifying implications.

Suddenly, everyone bolted for the exit.

I raced home. With pistol drawn, I entered my apartment. Pointing the pistol at my snoring wife's head, I said, "Wake up, Helen. Whadda ya say we run over to the hospital X-Ray Department? We won't stay long. Afterward, we can have breakfast at Denny's...maybe."

A BEAUTIFUL DOG EVERY TIME

Billions of TV watchers will never forget that fateful Super Bowl Sunday.

During a commercial break, the TV screen was filled with the magnificent countenance of Miss New World Order. The entire globe was astounded when she announced, "Here's something new! A miracle of the New World Order! Jiffy-Dog! A dog in every box!"

Popping the top of a blue box, she exclaimed, "Just pour the powder inside this box into a bucket, like I'm doing. Don't worry if you spill some. It wipes up easily. Now, add a gallon of water. Stir three times...and...Jiffy-Dog! A beautiful dog every time."

The screen split into a dozen panels showing men, women, and children pouring Jiffy-Dog into buckets. Suddenly, magnificent, fully-grown dogs of various breeds appeared in every one.

"Stay tuned for the next commercial break when I'll tell you more about this incredible and exciting new product," she proclaimed through glowing white teeth.

I'd never felt so excited. Instant dog. Just add water. What a fabulous concept.

It seemed forever until the next commercial break. Once again, the Jiffy-Dog hawker stirred the hearts and souls of the world's Super Bowl fans.

"Jiffy-Dog. The miracle product. A dog in every box. Tired of cleaning up doggie diamond? Tired of hearing dogs bark at nothing during the night, waking you from a sound sleep? Tired of them eating you out of house and home? Try Jiffy-Dog. The instant dog that doesn't eat, sleep, whine, chew your slippers, or have scatological accidents. Keep your fire hydrants spic and span. Keep bad doggie breath away. Stop dog bites forever, and save court costs. No more unwanted puppies. Jiffy-Dog. A dog in every box."

By the time the next commercial was presented, the only people on Earth not watching TV were in comas, catatonic states, or solitary confinement.

Miss New World Order demonstrated how to use a Jiffy-Dog dehydrator. The owner attached the gadget to the dog's snout, threw a switch, and the dog collapsed into a small pile of squishy material. The next day, the owner sprinkled some treated liquid—available for a nominal extra charge—on the material, and the dog expanded to its proper size, shape, color, and texture.

Ten million boxes of Jiffy-Dog sold the first day.

One billion were sold by the end of the week.

I bought one. Luckily, I got the extra-strength model that told a million jokes. Funniest one-liners I ever heard.

My instant dog was the best companion I ever had. Not only could he do amazing tricks and tell jokes, but he also watched TV ballgames with me, something my wife never did.

A month later, reports started to trickle in. Real dogs were disappearing. Investigative journalists filmed some sleeping under bridges and others in soup lines at rescue missions.

Congress attempted to pass legislation to protect abandoned real dogs. They failed, especially when the Leaders of the House, Senate, and the President switched to Jiffy-Dog.

Eventually, real dogs disappeared from the face of the Earth. Nobody cared. We had Jiffy-Dog.

Then came Jiffy-Cat.

And Jiffy-Wife.

DIGITAL IMAGES

I burst into the sheriff's office.

His face was buried in a paperback.

"What's the Speak-To-Authority Fee, here?" I asked, gasping for air.

"Ten bucks."

"I only have a twenty."

"Hell. Just as I was about to find out who dunnit. Couldn't you have come here five minutes later?"

"Sorry," I said, as he gave me change.

"Identify yourself," he snapped.

I did an about-face and unlatched the metal flap covering my buttocks. I could feel a slight sting as he waved a wand over both cheeks.

When the printer chimed, I closed the flap and turned around to face him.

"You're clean," he said, glancing at the hardcopy. "So, what brings you to Vermont?"

"I'm taking digital images of the autumn foliage. Been wanting to do this for years."

"Says here you're licensed for five hundred. How many images have you recorded? "

Closing my eyes, I pressed the tip of my nose. The digits 367 appeared in bright green in my mind's eye. I told him.

"And if I check your memory card right now, that's the count I'll get?"

"Yes, Sheriff. Honest. I know there's a big fine if I exceed the limit."

"In this town, it's jail for exceeding the limit. On everything. So why're you here bugging me?"

"Something terrible happened when I was in the woods snapping images. Just as I was about to take a close up of an orange leaf, a gun went off. The first shot whizzed by my ear. I hit the ground fast. Then a guy came tearing through the woods. Two other guys were chasing him. They got him in a back. Shot him three times. They were far enough away they didn't see me."

"Did they leave the body there?"

"Yeah, after they cut off his ears. After a while, I looked at the body. Didn't touch him, though. I know enough not to mess with a murder victim."

"Murder victim?" He looked at me sourly. "You're assuming a hell of a lot."

"Isn't gunning down somebody in the back who's running away, murder in this State?"

"It depends. What was this guy? Alien, android, automaton, human, humanoid, humanesque, mid-species, mutant, subspecies, robot, robotoid?"

"Couldn't tell. He was lying on his back. I didn't want to turn him over and scan his buttocks. Didn't wanna do anything that might contaminate the body and affect the outcome of the investigation."

"What about his face? See anything unusual?"

"Yeah. The letter N was tattooed on his forehead."

"Did he have red hair?"

"Yeah."

"Oh, him. Forget it. He was a nonconformist. I issued a hunting license to get him just the other day. There's no crime here. This was a sanctioned and licensed elimination."

"May I ask what he did?"

"The man just wouldn't conform. On Wednesday Sabbath, he refused to worship oak tree bark. Wiseass. As if that wasn't bad enough, he started going around whispering about maple trees being more worthy of worship because of their sweet sap. Created a stir. We can't have citizens questioning established religion. Where would this civilization be without rigid conformity?"

"Nowhere," I said.

"Did you take any digital images of him?"

"Yeah."

"How many?"

I pressed the tip of my nose twice, and the images scanned through my mind. "Eleven."

"I want them erased. Give me your digital memory card."

I twisted both ears forward two clicks. The sheriff reached over to the side of my head and yanked out the memory card.

"I see you got some great shots of the trees around the kissing bridge. The City Council would certainly approve these. Mind if I make a few copies?"

"No. Go ahead."

"Well, lookie here. I don't know if I like this image, the way you took a shot underneath a leaf with the sun coming through. Nobody around here would look at a leaf that way and record the image. It's too different, too unusual. Maybe you're a damn nonconformist. Maybe I oughta tattoo an N on your forehead."

"No. Wait. I am a conformist. I'm the best conformist in my town. I won the Big C Award last year. Just check with the town sheriff in Santa Buffoona, California. He'll tell you. I recite out loud all the slogans before I get up in the morning and before going to sleep at night. I adjust my behavior immediately with every new law. I act like the group, think like the group, worship like the group."

He stared, then said, "You're an out-of-stater. I could dummy up your memory card to show you worshiping maple tree bark. Claim that you're an apostle of the redhead. I could even issue a hunting license today. You'd be dead by tomorrow."

On the verge of panic, I blurted, "How much is a hunting license to bag nonconformists?"

"A thousand bucks."

"I'd like to donate a thousand to your benevolent fund. Use it as you think best."

"You wouldn't happen to have two thousand, would you?"

"Actually I have three thousand in traveler's checks. Would you accept them from a grateful, conforming citizen?"

"Sure thing," he chuckled. "Meanwhile, I'm gonna erase all the autumn foliage images from your memory card. I'll mail you some of the approved images our townsfolk have already taken."

"Wonderful. Nothing I'd like better than having the correct images of Vermont's autumn splendor. May I use all five eyes when viewing them?"

"Better check with your local Sheriff."

BLESS YOU, DR. PAVLOV

"Your Honor," Frank said, "I didn't know that being a resident of Santa Buffoona meant I had to buy one medium pizza a week from the Mayor's restaurant. Nobody ever told me."

"Ignorance is no excuse," said the judge. "Normally, I'd make an exception, but you're in arrears for $360. Considering a medium pizza costs $12—a bargain in my estimation—that means you've willfully disobeyed the laws of this city for thirty weeks straight."

"Even if I knew about the law, Your Honor, I'd have to plead for an exemption. Pizza makes me violently sick. Even a whiff of it makes me heave my guts out. Besides that, being forced to order a pizza every week is just about the dumbest law I ever heard of. I thought I lived in America, not some backwater dictatorship."

"Your medical problems are not the concerns of the city of Santa Buffoona. And I don't like your attitude about city ordinances passed by our esteemed city council, of which my son is a member. You are hereby sentenced to thirty weeks confinement at the Santa Buffoona Pizza Reeducation Center. One week for every week you've failed to purchase and consume a pizza." The judge banged his gavel and yelled, "Next case!"

Frank was taken away in chains.

When he arrived at the Pizza Reeducation Center, he noticed the odor of freshly baked pizza. He became violently ill and threw up on the two bruisers who escorted him. One of them thumped Frank's head with a billy club.

When Frank awoke, he found himself strapped to a table. Surrounding him were several people in costumes. One looked like a mushroom. Others looked like a piece of pepperoni, ball of cheese, giant tomato, and slice of pizza. Only their faces, arms, and legs showed.

"Why are you people dressed like a bunch of loonies?" Frank asked.

"I've never witnessed such hostility," the guy in the mushroom outfit said to the others. "He doesn't realize how much we love him."

"It's a shame," said the woman in a pepperoni costume. "Well, we have the cure for that, don't we?"

"Yes," said the cheese. "Okay, on the count of three, let's tell him how much we love him. One...two...three..."

"WE LOVE YOU!"

"And I HATE YOU, you stupid freaks! You should see how dumb you look dressed in those goofy outfits."

"Let's begin our loving treatments," said the slice of pizza.

The tomato forced Frank's mouth open while the mushroom guy squeezed pizza sauce from an eyedropper into his throat. Frank heaved again.

"Better get used to it," the pepperoni said. "You're gonna get ten drops every hour around the clock for the next thirty weeks."

The guy dressed like a ball of cheese approached and covered Frank's face with a cloth. He sprayed something onto the cloth that smelled cheesy. "Inhale deeply," he ordered.

Frank held his breath.

"Besides ingesting sauce, you'll sniff pizza cheese every hour. Now inhale, or we'll put you in solitary confinement. But remember: no matter what happens, we love you."

Frank inhaled, and immediately passed out.

He woke in time for the next treatment. As he was vomiting, he heard one of them say something about Dr. Pavlov, the Russian neurologist, and his methods of modifying behavior.

As the days wore on, Frank thought he was dying. But at the start of the tenth week, the vomiting suddenly stopped. And by the end of the fifteenth week, he found himself salivating and looking forward to his next feeding. He also began to feel affection for his re-educators.

"You're responding very nicely," the pepperoni said. "Dr. Pavlov would've been proud of you. Starting at midnight, we're going to double the amounts of pizza sauce and cheese aroma. Don't forget how much we love you."

At the end of week 26, Frank could hardly wait for his hourly doses.

During week 27, they substituted morsels of freshly baked pepperoni pizza topped with mushrooms and extras sauce and cheese. Frank was surprised how good it tasted. His re-educators applauded when he didn't vomit.

When week 28 began, they gave him a large slice of pepperoni pizza every hour. The first time they did this, Frank experienced a colossal orgasm when he bit into the pizza. The same thing happened during the next feeding. Frank found himself begging them to change the feeding times to every thirty minutes instead of every hour. The re-educators changed the schedule to accommodate Frank's cravings.

"Bless you, Dr. Pavlov," Frank moaned every time he ate pizza and was hurled into paroxysms of frenzied delight.

When Frank was released, he was brought before the judge.

"Have you learned your lesson?" the judge asked.

"Yes, Your Honor."

"From now on, will you willingly and cheerfully observe our city's laws, especially the one that requires you to purchase and consume one medium pizza per week?"

"Absolutely."

"Do you have anything to say for the court record?"

"Yes, Your Honor. Is there any chance of you giving me a life sentence in the Pizza Reeducation Center?"

PUPPY ISLAND

There once was a youngster named Harold who lived on a beautiful Island in the middle of the Pacific Ocean.

Harold and his family and everyone else who lived there thought they were puppies, because their homeland was named Puppy Island. But they weren't puppies. They were really giant cockroaches. If they had been puppies, they would've had fairy godmothers to tell them exactly what they were. But unlike every other living thing on Earth, giant cockroaches didn't have fairy godmothers to tell them anything. Why that was so was one of the greatest mysteries of the Universe.

Puppy Islanders were always deeply depressed. Nobody knew why. Everyday upon awakening they'd ask themselves and everyone around them, "Why do we feel so blue? Aren't puppies always supposed to be happy? But we never are. How can that be?"

The truth was that giant cockroaches by their very nature were depressed. It was the way they were created. Elsewhere on Earth where giant cockroaches lived, the situation was the same. Since many of them inhabited faraway lands where puppies also lived, the cockroaches asked the puppies for a favor. "Since you guys are lucky enough to have fairy godmothers, please ask them why we giant cockroaches are always so miserably down-hearted."

The puppies' fairy godmothers all gave the same answer: "Some things are happy all the time, and some aren't. You should've been born puppies instead of giant cockroaches. Then you'd always be happy."

But Puppy Island was isolated from the rest of the world, so Harold, his family, and all the other residents never learned this.

One day when Harold was playing on the beach, some scientists came ashore in a rowboat. They asked him to take them to the King. Though surprised to see other living things who didn't look like him, Harold complied.

King Puppy The Twenty-Third was amazed to see living things, who weren't puppies, standing before him. Nevertheless, he welcomed them.

"We the puppies of this great land offer you our blessings and hospitality. From whence have you come?"

"America."

"Where's that?"

"Far away."

"How did you get here?"

"On an aircraft carrier."

Their intriguing answers led to a long discussion in which the scientists informed the King that he and his subjects weren't puppies.

"Nonsense!" shouted the King. "Prove it!"

"Okay," said the scientists, "we'll conduct a test."

When the King agreed, the scientists asked to be taken to the island's highest hill. They also asked that all inhabitants of the island gather at the bottom.

The next day, King Puppy accompanied the scientists to the hill. When reaching the top, the scientists threw 10,000 Frisbees toward the sky. All sailed through the air for a while, then fell to the ground.

"If you were puppies," said a scientist, "everyone at the bottom of this hill would've chased the Frisbees, caught them before they landed, and returned them to us. The only things in the world that don't chase Frisbees are giant cockroaches. Therefore, you and your subjects are giant cockroaches, not puppies."

Though utterly astonished, everyone believed the scientists. But that didn't end their depression.

"We can help you get rid of depression," a scientist said. We've invented a thermonuclear device called a Happy Bomb. If you'll let us explode one over your island, everyone will start laughing. But we don't know for how long. The only residents of this island who won't be happy afterward will be those who don't eat corn flakes for breakfast."

The King agreed to the test. He figured two good things would happen if the test succeeded. First, everyone would finally feel happy for a while. Second, he could rid the island of imprisoned criminals. Annual costs for their care and feeding drained billions from the national treasury —-a most depressing situation.

The date was set. The King chose Harold to pull the string that would detonate the nuclear bomb, as it floated five hundred feet overhead in a hot air balloon.

The King ordered all his subjects, except prisoners, to eat corn flakes for breakfast.

When Harold pulled the string, a brilliant flash and gigantic noise raced halfway around the world. Everyone was dumbfounded by the huge, colorful, mushroom cloud that formed and reached high into the sky.

Suddenly, everyone except the dead prisoners started laughing. Their laughter lasted six months without letup. But when they stopped, they felt terribly depressed once again.

After much deep thought, Harold got an idea. He went to the King and said, "If you will build boats, make me a Prince, and give me a thousand followers, we will row to America and steal their Happy Bombs. Then we will be able to laugh again."

"Brilliant idea!" said the King.

Prince Harold and his men went to America, stole all the Happy Bombs, and arrived home safely.

The next day, Harold set off another bomb over the island. Everyone started laughing again, except the newest batch of prisoners who died because they were denied corn flakes for breakfast.

This time, everyone on Puppy Island laughed continuously for a whole year.

Afterward, Harold met with the King. While giggling, he said, "Now that we have the secret of creating and sustaining perpetual happiness, we can eliminate sadness throughout the world forever by exploding our Happy Bombs over every nation. Allow us to do this, and you'll be famous and forever beloved by all the inhabitants of the Earth."

The King heartily approved Harold's plan. He also approved Harold's idea of changing the island's name to Ha-Ha Island.

Harold and his men secretly setup Happy Bombs over every nation on Earth. To celebrate the King's birthday, Harold gave him a very, very long string that was connected to all the bombs around the globe.

"Happy Birthday," his subjects cried, as the King pulled the string.

And that is why everyone in the world is always so happy, the word depression has disappeared from dictionaries, and so many nations have thermonuclear bombs.

CREAMIES

"Defend yourselves! The Creamies are coming!" somebody yelled through a bullhorn from a passing car.

"What's a Creamie?" I yelled. But it was too late. The car was already down the block.

I turned on the TV. A grim-faced Exalted Chairman of the Amalgamated States of America was addressing the nation.

"To repeat," said the Exalted Chairman. "At precisely 7:17 PM Eastern Time, every one of our seventy-two states was invaded by an unknown number of hostile forces. We believe they parachuted from stealth transports. Preliminary reports indicate they now control the following states: Florida, Missouri, Calimexico, Idaho, Greenwich, and Pomerania. All National Guard and Reserve forces are hereby ordered to report to their assembly areas, immediately. With the help of the Eternal Godhead, we will prevail. Long live the Amalgamated States of America."

"What's going on, Honey?" my wife, Betsy, asked as she came into the family room.

"The day we've been dreading all our lives has arrived," I said, grabbing an assault rifle from my gun cabinet.

"You mean nuclear war?"

"It's not nuclear yet. But we've been invaded by a foreign army. I just saw the Exalted Chairman on TV. He said all seventy-two states have been invaded. And somebody just passed in a car yelling through a bullhorn that the Creamies were coming."

"Who are they?" she asked.

"He didn't say. He probably meant those bastard Creamonians in Antarctica who've been threatening us for decades. I'm gonna go outside and check around."

The woods were only a block away. When I reached the perimeter, I heard autumn leaves crunching. Scanning the area with night vision binoculars, I spotted something that startled me. Hundreds of huge, puffy looking blobs were heading toward me. They reminded me of gigantic jelly donuts. Then it struck me: maybe the Creamies were cream-filled donuts.

I wondered how effective my rifle would be, considering donuts are soft and mushy inside—especially the cream-filled ones. Selecting a target through my sniper scope, I fired. Good grief! It kept moving forward as if nothing happened. Yet, I saw the gaping wound the bullet had torn in its side. I panicked and raced home.

"CNN said they've captured ten more states," Betsy said, as I rushed through the front door.

"I just shot one, but he didn't even fall down. You ain't gonna believe this, but I'm pretty sure they're giant cream-filled donuts. They got no heads, arms or legs. What the hell can we use to fight crazed cream donuts?"

She answered by screaming hysterically.

I slapped her to bring her around. "If you don't get yourself together, we're gonna die," I said. "I need you to be strong. Got any ideas on how we can stop them?"

"Dilute them. When you put cream in your coffee, you dilute the strength of the coffee. We need something to dilute their cream filling. Maybe water will work."

"You're brilliant!" I said. "But how can we get water inside them?"

"Fill them full of bullet holes," she said. "Which do you wanna be? Shooter or water sprayer?"

"Whatever you prefer," I said. "It's your idea."

"Nothing I'd like better than to blast them full of holes," she said, grabbing my rifle and night vision equipment. I'll get on the roof and fire from there."

As she climbed the roof, I went out front and stretched the garden hose as far as it would go. I tied a high-powered LED flashlight to the hose for illumination, and attached a high-powered spray nozzle. Then, I moved the car to the street to use as a shield.

Suddenly I heard shots. "Here they come," Betsy hollered.

I couldn't understand how Creamies could move around without legs or feet. But then snakes don't have any, and they get around pretty damn fast.

When the first Creamy got close, I aimed the nozzle and sprayed. The impact knocked the Creamy to the ground. I rushed toward it, blasting the bullet wounds with water. In seconds, its mushy cream innards turned into thin white liquid that flooded the street. As the thing breathed its last, it emitted an ear-piercing scream.

They attacked continuously for two hours. None ever got past my car.

When the battle was over, we counted 462 dead donuts.

Betsy called Homeland Security and told them how we whipped the Creamies. They spread our battle technique throughout the nation. The tide of battle quickly turned in America's favor.

Three million cream filled donuts were destroyed that night. The nation's cats had the time of their lives lapping six million gallons of diluted cream from the nation's streets.

The Exalted Chairman presented us with hero medals for helping the nation defeat the Creamies.

* * * *

One hundred stories below Area 51, a scientist made entries into his research journal.

"Too bad cream didn't work," he mumbled. "I really wanted to become Emperor of the Amalgamated States by the end of the week."

He went to the eight-foot, doughy blob strapped to a table and sprinkled it with electrified powdered sugar. Then he checked the steel tubes running from the blob to the ceiling. Certain all was ready, he threw a switch and screamed manically, "Time to try blueberry jelly."

A BIG STOCKHOLDER

"I can't understand what you're saying," Burns told the humanoid.

The creature twisted his nose and pulled both ears twice to activate his voice translator. "Can you understand me now?"

"Yeah. So, what can I do for you Mr—"

"Glixi. I understand you find lost things. Is that true?"

"Depends on what it is. What did you lose?"

"My youth."

Burns grabbed a bottle of cheap whiskey and took a big swig. "Where do you think it happened?"

"Zip-Mart."

"Which one? There's so damn many of them."

"The one on the dark side of the Moon."

"Ah well, that explains it all," Burns said. "It's so dark up there, folks are liable to lose anything. In fact, they often do. So, I assume you want me to find it?"

"Yeah. I'm not having fun being old."

"I know what you mean," Burns said, pointing to his own white hair. "So, how old are you really? I mean before you lost your youth at Zip-Mart?"

"Four."

"Oh brother! You sure lost it in a big way. I don't blame you for wanting it back. I'll take your case on a contingency basis. You pay only when I recover your youth. Well, I mean your parents will have to pay, because when you get your youth back, you'll only be four. What's your phone number? I'll call them to see if they agree."

"I don't know. Remember, I was only four years old."

Burns was unable to find the parent's phone number through his computer. Sunspots were causing havoc with interplanetary data retrieval systems.

"I can't get their number right now. But I'll take your case. I'm sure your parents will pay when they see you back home safe and sound and your proper age. So, for starters, can you remember what you were doing in Zip-Mart right before you discovered you'd suddenly grown old?"

"Yeah. My mom strapped me in a shopping cart. Then we went to the deli counter. She ordered a pound of green Moon cheese. I started whining because I was bored. After that, she took me into the ladies rest room. That's the last thing I remember until I found myself in the baggage compartment of the Earth Shuttle. When it landed I discovered I was here in Los Angeles. And very old."

"This case is gonna be easier to solve than I expected," said Burns.

"Really?"

"Yep. I figure the Wicked Witch of the Stalls stole your youth. It wouldn't have happened if your mom had put you in the men's room. But I understand her reluctance, considering the Moon's full of sleaze bags. You see, this particular witch is extremely resentful of the male gender. And you trod on her territory. To her, that's a king-size no-no. You're lucky she didn't turn you into a frog."

"I oughta sue Zip-Mart for letting her lurk around the ladies room."

"Don't bother. You can't possibly win. She owns ten million shares. That's lotsa clout. No way will they let you lock horns with a big shareholder like her. Okay, I'll catch the shuttle, go up there, and find your lost youth. Gimme your address so I know where to return it. By the way, I suggest you go back on the same flight with me. When you arrive, call your mom to explain the situation. Otherwise, when you get home, she'll scream her head off when you try to get into the house. She won't realize you're her little Glixi who's grown so very old. She might think you're a home invader, or worse."

They departed on the shuttle, and went their separate ways when they arrived on the dark side of the Moon.

Burns took a cab to Zip-Mart. On the way, he tried to figure a way of getting into the ladies room without getting arrested. Didn't take long for him to work out a scheme.

Inside the store, he headed for the women's department. He found a dress that flattered his tall, thin frame, plus a big-feathered straw hat that was all the rage on that side of the Moon.

Entering the ladies room to the sound of multiple flushes, he noticed the Wicked Witch of the Stalls staring into a mirror and squeezing pimples. Next to her was a duffel bag marked LOST YOUTH. Pulling a blackjack from his pocket, Burns slammed her head from behind. As she crumpled to the floor, he grabbed the bag and rushed out.

While hurrying toward the main exit, he checked inside the bag and found a bunch of small boxes. Each bore a name. Finding Glixi's, he stuffed the box into his pocket.

At the front of the store, he noticed several loitering old timers.

"Hey...anybody here lost their youth?"

Six toothless mouths responded.

"Maybe it's in one of these boxes," Burns said, dumping the bag's contents onto the floor. "See if your name's on any of them."

While Burns hailed a taxi, a seven-year-old boy ran toward him. "Thanks for finding my lost youth, Mister," he said.

Arriving at Glixi's residence, he knocked on the door. When Glixi opened it, Burns gave him the box.

"Thanks a lot. You found this so fast. You're worth every penny. My dad said if this works, he'll put a check in the mail, tonight."

Burns told Glixi to pour the box's contents into his left ear. Suddenly, a four-year-old stood where an old white-haired man had been moments earlier.

Burns was on the Earth Shuttle before the witch awoke. She never knew what hit her. Nor did she have a clue as to the whereabouts of all the youth she'd stolen.

He decided to never again enter a Zip-Mart ladies room for any reason. Just in case the Wicked Witch of the Stalls had relatives who were also wicked, witchy, man-haters, and big Zip-Mart stockholders.

THE GREATEST FLAMENCO DANCER IN ALL FLYDOM

"Members of the jury," said the giant horse fly. "Before you stands a most despicable example of the human species: a serial fly killer. According to sworn testimony, he's murdered 5,322 of our noble brethren."

"Is this true," asked the praying mantis in black robes sitting at the judge's bench.

"Yes," I said.

"Tell the court how you committed these evil deeds," said the horse fly.

"With a fly swatter."

"Hear that?" yelled the prosecuting attorney. "He just admitted using a FLY SWATTER! One of the most horrid assault weapons ever invented. So deadly in fact, that it was banned fifty years ago by the Amalgamated Insect Nations. This evil human hid one in his basement during the Fly Swatter Confiscation of 2009. Then he used it to dispatch well over five thousand of our brethren. The fact that he hid a weapon of mass destruction in defiance of the AIN is proof of malicious intent to commit premeditated murder on an unheard of scale. I'd go so far as to say he had genocide in mind."

"I've never seen a fly swatter," said the judge. "Do you have one to show us?"

"Yes. But I must warn you, it's not a sight for weak stomachs."

"Do all members of the jury feel you can handle this? If not, I'll have the bailiff distribute barf bags. Let me see the hands of those who think they'll need them."

Several fly legs shot up.

After the bags were distributed, the prosecuting attorney removed a plastic fly swatter from a locked case. It was stained with fly blood and guts. When he showed it to the jury, many regurgitated, including some without barf bags.

The judge had to order a fifteen-minute recess.

During the break, I thought about all the flies I'd killed. In my mind, I hadn't killed enough of those disease-carrying bastards.

When the trial resumed, the horsefly said, "According to eyewitnesses, you killed a fly that landed on your salami sandwich. What you killed that day was the greatest Flamenco dancer in all of Flydom. If you had taken the time to notice his arrival, you would've seen that he'd come merely to entertain you. What many have paid high prices to see, he wanted to perform for you free of charge. And do you know why?

Because he loved mankind. He was an incredibly altruistic insect who merely wished to entertain you. And how did you repay him? You chased him around a room from which he was unable to escape. When you cornered him, you smashed him with this fly swatter. Didn't you hear his screams when you wounded him? Sworn testimony says you didn't even bother to call for medical assistance. Nor did you show the slightest remorse when he died. You, Sir, have not a shred of compassion in your being."

"But that day I got real sick from the germs he deposited on my sandwich," I said. "Not to mention I was hospitalized for three years because of a nasty staph infection. By killing him, I rid the human world of a filthy, germy beast."

Sounds of shock came from the jury.

"I see no need to pursue this case any further," said the prosecuting attorney. "The defendant has just admitted his guilt. Not only that, he's insulted our allies, the Germs, by making false and ridiculous claims about infection. I ask the jury to do its sacred duty and return a guilty verdict for mass murder. Further, I plead with the jury to recommend the death penalty. The sooner this vermin is removed from our midst, the safer the entire insect world will be."

The judge ordered the jury to a deliberation room. They returned in thirty seconds, saying I was guilty of murder and hate crimes in the first degree on all 5,322 counts.

"I sentence you to death, " said the judge. "Tomorrow at sunrise, you will thrown into a shark tank where you will be dismembered until pronounced dead. May the Lord of The Flies condemn you to the Pit, and may your miserable soul burn in Hell fire for eternity."

Suddenly the courtroom door burst open. In came the Emperor of the Cockroaches.

"I demand to be heard," he said. "I've been watching these proceedings on television."

"You may speak," said the judge.

"This man is just as altruistic as the Flamenco dancer he killed. He's done magnificent things for the subjects of my empire without asking anything in return. For one, he deliberately avoided cleaning his house, leaving scraps of food and garbage everywhere. He did this for years. These charitable acts allowed us to obtain free room and board for millions for our kind in his humble abode. Therefore, I ask for leniency."

After pondering a minute, the judge said, "Let it never be said that this court is not merciful. I hereby change the sentence. I now sentence you to be ground into crumb-sized pieces, and then fed to homeless and orphaned cockroaches. Does the prisoner have anything to say?"

"Yes. This court is a travesty. I didn't even have a defense attorney."

"Serial killers don't have the right to a defense attorney. Let's not waste any more time. Remove the prisoner, transport him to the meat grinder, and carry the sentence."

With as much strength as I could muster, I punched the bailiff, then rushed to the table where the fly swatter lay. Grabbing it, I swung with all my might. I killed a jury member on the first smack and the judge on the second.

When I headed for the window to escape, the Emperor of the Cockroaches yelled, "Don't do it. They'll send killer hornets to hunt you down. The meat grinder would be faster and less painful."

"I'll take my chances," I said, crashing through the window with the swatter in hand.

I had to fight my way through fly-infested streets. I don't know how many of the bastards I decimated before I spotted a huge swarm of killer hornets heading toward me. Before they attacked, I dropped the swatter and surrendered to the AIN police.

They shackled me and threw into an armored car.

As they led me down the path to the meat grinder, I lost my nerve and began to tremble. But my terror dissipated when the Emperor of the Cockroaches called my name and said, "Michael, your death will not be in vain. It has profound existential meaning to my subjects. Because of you, this very day, millions of homeless and orphaned cockroaches will enjoy a wonderfully nutritious meal."

TELL YOU WHAT I'M GONNA DO

"Hey, Kid, give it a try. Ten chances for a dollar. Toss a ping-pong ball in the basket. If it stays in, you win the best prizes on the Midway."

"But your shelves are empty. Where are the prizes?"

"In your head."

"Whadda ya mean?"

"If you win, you get whatever you want. Name it, and you got it. But you gotta tell me within one second after the ball settles in the basket. If you take longer, you lose."

"I bet if I win and say Mustang convertible, you'll give me a little toy car."

"No way. See all those trailers parked over there? They're loaded with prizes. New cars. Designer clothes. Gold jewelry. Anything a teenager like you could ever want. You name it, I got it."

"You're kidding."

"Nope. See that gal in the tight red jeans at the hot dog stand? She won a solid-gold watch a few minutes ago. Ask her to show it to you."

"Excuse me, Lady. The guy over there said you won a gold watch from him. Is that true?"

"Yep. Look at this beauty. I'll bet it's worth ten thousand bucks. I won it on my eighth try."

"Wow! I'm gonna go back there and see if I can win a car."

"Good luck," she said.

"I see you're back. How many balls do you want?"

"Ten."

"Here you go. Good luck."

"Hey! I won!"

"Forfeit," he said. "You didn't name your prize within a second."

"Aw hell. Well, watch closely, because I'm gonna win again. Yahoo! BUBBLE GUM."

"We got a winaaaa! Here's a piece of bubble gum, Kid. Chew it in good health."

"Wait. Something weird just happened. I was gonna say Mustang convertible, but somehow I ended up saying bubble gum. That sure as hell ain't gonna happen again. Gimme ten more balls."

"Here you go. Good luck. Hey, don't lean over the counter like that. It's against the rules."

"Sorry. Okay...watch this. PLASTIC COMB.

"We got a winaaaa! You're a very lucky kid. Here's a nice comb for your curly hair."

"Dammit! It happened again. I don't know why I said plastic comb instead of Mustang convertible."

"You must be over excited. Tell you what I'm gonna do. Next time you win, I'll name the prize for you."

"Really?"

"I swear. What color convertible do you want?

"Candy apple red."

"Okay, Kid. Win again, and I'll name it for you."

"Damn! I can't seem to get any balls in the basket."

"Maybe you'll get lucky with the next one."

"Hey! I won!"

"Your immortal soul," he said

"What? You were supposta say Mustang convertible."

"Sorry. My mistake. Tell you what I'm gonna do. Whadda ya say we make a trade. I'll give you a Mustang convertible right now for your immortal soul."

"What's that?"

"Nothing compared to a beautiful new car. Think of all the hot chicks you'll be able to pickup. Is it a deal?"

"Hell yeah."

"We got another winaaaa!"

THE WOMAN WITHOUT THE RED DRESS

Downhearted and dejected, Harvey walked into the police station. The moment he told them what he'd done, he knew they'd book him. The trial would be swift. The jury would find him guilty. And he'd be executed for his horrible crime. He shuddered. But deep inside he knew it was the right thing to do. No sense trying to hide it.

"I'm the one who did it. I'm guilty," he said to the Desk Sergeant, eyes downcast.

"What did you do?"

"I killed her."

"Her who?" the Sergeant asked roughly, pressing a button under his desk to alert detectives.

"The woman without the red dress."

"Where's the body?" the cop asked glancing at last night's list of major crimes.

"I don't remember."

It had been a rare night: no murders had been listed on the Detroit Police Blotter.

"What's your name?"

"Harvey Clutch."

"Your address and phone number?"

Harvey gave both, then added, "I'm sorry. I didn't mean to do it. But I get such overwhelming urges. Aren't you going to read me my rights?"

"Not today. We skip it every other day. Gives citizens a break. Tell you what I'll do. I'll call you as soon as we find the body. Did you say she wasn't in a green dress?"

"No. Red. Found it in my bed next to me when I woke up. Empty. I mean she wasn't in it."

"I see. You humped her and then she left without her dress."

"Yeah, that's right. Raped her fifteen times."

A side door opened. "I'm Detective Hobs," said a nasty-looking brute. "Need to talk to me, do you?"

The Sergeant winked. "No need. He just confessed to rape. And murder. I've taken his statement. He's guilty as sin. I just told him to go home until we find the body. You know, the woman who was murdered last night? The one without her red dress?"

"Oh her. Well, we just got in a new bunch of stiffs. All women. One of them didn't have a red dress. They're still dusting her thingee for prints. Soon as we find your prints on the body, we'll call you. Can you get here within fifteen minutes after we call? Or will you need to eat first?"

"Oh no. I snack quite often during the day. Diabetic. I'll be down here right after you call."

"OK," said Hobs. "Meanwhile, don't skip town. We'll be watching the busses, trains, and airports."

"Oh, I won't try to run."

"OK, then," said the Sergeant. "I'll see you as soon as we get a make on your prints. Probably in a couple hours."

"Should I pack a little bag before I come in?"

"Nah. We have everything here. The best brands. We'll take good care of you."

"That's very thoughtful. I don't deserve it. I'm guilty, you know?"

"Yep. I know. And we're gonna throw the book at you."

"Thanks. I deserve it. OK. I'll see you later."

"Bye-Bye," said the Sergeant.

"Toodle-oo," said the detective.

When Harvey left, they pissed their pants laughing.

The Sarge added Harvey's name and general description to their list of obsessive confessors.

Such nice guys, Harvey said to himself. It's gratifying to see my tax dollars at work.

Back in his basement apartment, Harvey removed the red dress from his bed, put it on a hangar, and hung it in a closet. Then, using a black marking pen, he wrote "PEOPLE'S EXHIBIT NO. 1," on a 3 x 5 card and stapled it to the dress.

Popping a Coke can, he tried to remember where he'd stashed her body. He checked the park for freshly dug holes on his way home. Didn't see any. He was certain he put her behind the oak tree. The one with all the initials carved into the trunk. Or had he been dreaming?

She wasn't in the oven, or the clothes dryer. Not in the bathtub, either.

That's odd. I thought there was a woman here last night. Or was that a dream?

When he checked under his bed he saw her decapitated head and the rest of her body. He also found the flexible straw through which he'd slowly swigged her blood. It looked reusable, so he rinsed it and left it out to dry.

Grabbing another 3 x 5 card, he carefully wrote, "PEOPLE'S EXHIBIT NO. 2," and stapled it to her pallid cheek. "PEOPLE'S EXHIBIT NO. 3," was stapled to her groin. The one he'd bounced on so joyously after her decapitation. Fifteen times. Three times more than the last one. The one without the blue dress.

HIGHWAY 35

The cop vomited when he turned on his flashlight and looked inside the Lexus. When he gained his composure, he called his Sergeant.

"Sarge, you ain't gonna believe this. I stopped a car that was speeding and weaving on Highway 35. I figured a DUI. But when I looked inside, I saw—damn, you ain't gonna believe this—I saw a freakin' headless body in the driver's seat with its hands on the steering wheel. As if it was driving the car. It was wearing a cop's uniform. And if that ain't weird enough, there's a decapitated head in the passenger seat. I swear the damn thing smirked at me."

"Forget it, Walsh."

won't harm you "Whadda ya mean?"

"Just walk away from it."

"I don't get it. This is the weirdest thing I ever saw. An obvious crime, and you want me to walk away? Shouldn't I at least call a towing service?"

"You won't have to. And if you did, they'd only laugh at you."

"Sergeant Harding," said Walsh, "I don't want to sound disrespectful, but I don't think this is the time to joke around. There's a dead cop in the car's driver seat. He's been decapitated. Besides our department and the FBI, it sounds like something Homeland Security might be very interested in."

"Walsh, under normal circumstances, I'd dispatch a whole bunch of patrol cars and detectives to the scene. But take my word for it, I'd only be wasting my time. Just get back into your patrol car and move on. It's the Highway 35 Monster. It shows up every five years. Didn't anybody ever tell you about it when you joined the force?"

"No. You mean it's some kind of ghost?"

"That's what some call it. By the way, how long have you been there?"

"About five minutes."

"Better leave right away. Wait. Look inside again to check the cop's badge number. Then get the hell outta there. Once you leave, call in the number to me. If you know what's good for you, you'll get in your car and floor it."

Walsh went back to the Lexus and checked the badge.

He jumped when a voice said, "You could have asked me for my badge number. I would've told you."

"Who said that?" Walsh asked with a shaky voice.

"Me," said the head. "Why don't you get in the car and join us for a nice little drive to the cemetery."

Walsh never ran so fast. Within seconds his car was doing 80.

Trembling all over, he kept saying to himself, "It didn't happen....it didn't happen...it didn't happen."

Then he remembered the Sergeant wanted the body's badge number. He called and gave it.

"That badge used to belong to Bill Jones," said Harding. "He disappeared five years ago. I'll tell the Captain you found his, uh, body—or whatever it was. He'll understand. He believes in ghosts. Good thing you got out of there when you did."

"Why?"

"The legend says if you stay long enough or answer any questions the head asks, you end up headless and driving the car five years from now. Did the head ask you any questions?"

"Yeah."

"Like what?"

"It said, 'Why don't you get in the car and join us for a nice little drive to the cemetery.'"

"Hmm. I wonder what it asked Bill Jones. He musta stopped the same car five years ago when he disappeared. I guess he was dumb enough to answer."

"Are there any other legends I should know about that you guys forgot to tell me when I joined the force?"

"Yeah. There's one more. But it's so off-the-wall and horrible, I don't even want to mention it," said Harding.

Walsh had such terrifying dreams that night and for weeks afterward, he was unable to perform his duties properly. He kept seeing his headless body in the Lexus, driving down Highway 35. Even worse, he saw himself talking to his decapitated head on the seat next to him. Visits to the police psychiatrist didn't help.

Two months later, he resigned. Soon afterward, the nightmares stopped, and his anxieties began to dissipate.

But now he faced another problem: the economic turndown made jobs extremely difficult to find. Desperate to put beans on the table, Walsh felt extremely lucky to find a job selling balloons at the zoo. He couldn't understand why hundreds of people hadn't lined up to get the job, especially since it paid twenty dollars an hour plus commissions.

But then nobody ever told him the legend about the balloon seller and the ghost of the escaped gorilla.

NO REPRIEVE

Ron's cell phone rang as he staggered from the bar.

"Ron Biggs?" asked an ethereal-sounding voice.

"Yeah. Who wants to know?"

"Greetings," said the voice.

"Who the hell is this?"

"He who is feared by all."

"Up your kazoo, you freakin' jerk!" Ron yelled, then hung up.

His phone rang again.

"I will not be insulted or ignored," said the voice. "Don't hang up until you're told, or a taxi will jump the curb and cut you in half. Understand?"

Ron saw an out-of-service taxi suddenly go out of control and swerve toward him. "I understand!" he screamed.

The driver regained control, missing Ron by three feet.

"As you see, I mean what I say," the voice said.

"What the hell's going on? Who are you?"

"Destrudo."

The phone went silent. Realizing what'd just happened, Ron panicked and ran.

A cop stopped him. "What's the problem?"

"Nothing, Officer. I'm in a hurry to get home."

"You smell boozy. Better take a cab. It ain't healthy to be walking around here at night when you're drunk."

"I'll grab a cab soon as I can find one."

"There's plenty in the Theatre District."

"I'll go there right now," Ron said.

As Ron hurried away, his phone rang again.

"Better make your last confession," Destrudo said.

"I don't believe in that. In fact, I don't believe you exist."

"You soon will," said the voice. "I came to warn you...you're going to die in ten hours."

"Nonsense!"

"Ask a priest about me. Tell him Destrudo sent you. Or don't you dare?"

The line went dead.

St. Michael's, where Ron used to attend Alcoholics Anonymous meetings, was a few blocks away. Ron arrived just as a meeting ended. Spotting a Roman collar, he called, "Hey, Father."

"Can I help you?"

"I was told to find a priest."

"Who told you?"

"Destrudo."

Ron heard a sharp intake of breath.

"I can't help you," the priest said.

"Can you tell me who Destrudo is?"

"The Angel of Death."

"Aw c'mon," Ron said. "There's no such thing."

"Wrong. Once his sword is raised, nobody can evade his vicious attack. The time, place, and date were ordained before your birth. Have you lived a good life?"

"Sure. It's been real good grabbing anything I wanted before the other guy did."

"Even if it meant stealing and killing?"

"Yeah."

"Then you've lived an evil life."

"What's evil to you is ordinary to me."

"There's no reprieve," said the priest. "Prepare to face your maker."

"No!" Ron shouted. "I don't believe any of your hokum."

"You've been unreasonably privileged. Few have ever heard Destrudo's voice. Perhaps he'll grant the death you desire."

"How about this: suppose I ask to be whacked right between the eyes by a flying saucer while I'm standing on top of the Empire State Building, giving Destrudo the finger? At least I'll go out knowing for sure if flying saucers exist."

"Foolish sacrilege," said the priest.

When Ron hailed a cab, Destrudo called again. "You have nine hours."

"Is that so? How's it gonna happen?"

"It's a surprise."

"Hey, why not wipe me out in style? Do something spectacular that'll make the papers with headlines saying, 'Destrudo Strikes Again.' I'll go to the New York Times and tell a reporter what's gonna happen. I'll say that tomorrow morning, a flying saucer is gonna whack me while I'm standing on top of the Empire State Building."

"Is that how you prefer to be dispatched at 8:45 tomorrow morning?"

"Yep. Might as well go out with a big bang. It'll give people something to talk about for generations."

"Granted."

The phone went dead.

Ron decided to go the Times Building and tell his story to a reporter. He figured they might even pay him a few dollars that he could use to buy whiskey.

"On top of the Empire State Building?" asked a reporter.

"Yep."

"Can't happen there. The top floor's closed to visitors for the next two months. They're sandblasting the outside of the building to remove decades of soot. Why not go to the World Trade Center instead and wait on the observation tower? Let the flying saucer whomp you there."

"Great idea," Ron said.

The entire night crew of the Times was in stitches when the reporter told them about the zonked-out wacko and his impending death by flying saucer.

Next morning, as Ron rode the subway to the World Trade Center, Destrudo called and asked if he was ready to die.

"Yeah. But I changed my mind about the Empire State Building. The World Trade Center is higher and more spectacular. I'm going there now. I'll be standing outside on the observation tower waiting for the flying saucer."

"Wonderful choice," Destrudo replied. "That'll make it even easier for the saucer's pilot to see you."

Ron took the elevator to the World Trade Center's observation tower. While standing outside on the 110th floor scanning the skies for flying saucers, his phone rang.

"There's something I wanted to tell you before you die. Flying saucers don't exist. But, I've found a suitable alternative. Look to your right. See that airliner heading your way?"

BEFORE AND AFTER

Before zombies ambushed Santa Claus and ate every ounce of his brains, he lived in Tahiti, wore a grass skirt, was beardless, employed only human union members in his toy factories, used horses to pull a gift-filled tractor trailer, and delivered presents to children by entering their homes through the front door.

A team of doctors led by the renowned Dr. Frankenfutz, arranged for an immediate brain replacement.

The operation was a success. However, as soon as Santa was released from the Frankenfutz Institute for Brain Swaps, he moved to the Arctic, wore only red suits, grew a beard, employed only non-union elves in his factories, used reindeer to pull a gift-filled sleigh, and delivered presents to children by entering their homes through chimneys.

The world's greatest behavioral scientists, and even Dr. Sigmund Freud, were unable to explain his bizarre behavior.

After years of intense research in the Frankenfutz archives, the mystery of his radical behavioral changes has been solved. Turns out that Santa's new brain came from the village idiot.

DON'T MESS WITH SETI

Blurp and Glurp were bored. "I got an idea," said Glurp. "Let's play a trick on those jerky Earth guys who are always sending stupid radio signals throughout the galaxy. They're the laughingstock of the entire universe. They're actually hoping somebody will answer their transmissions. Maybe it's time somebody did, heh-heh."

Using their dad's radio transmitter, Glurp spoke into the microphone. "Can anybody on Earth hear me?"

"Yes!" said an excited scientist monitoring a radio telescope on Earth for SETI (Search for Extraterrestrial Intelligence). "Where are you?"

"Mars."

"This is amazing. We were starting to think no intelligent beings were out there. You're the first to contact us. Tell me something about yourself."

"Me and my brother love pepperoni pizza, but they don't make them here. Can you deliver an extra large one to us?" Giggling, Glurp turned off the transmitter.

The SETI scientist reported the Martian prankster to the FBI. They in turn notified President Striker. "I'll fix that Martian wise-ass!" said Striker. He asked the Director of Space Exploration if they had any rockets that looked like pepperoni pizzas."

"No," said the Director. "But we can get one ready by tomorrow."

When notified the rocket was ready for firing, Striker hollered, "Eat this, you Martian freak!" Then he pressed the LAUNCH button. A few hours later, Blurp and Glurp were amazed to see a pepperoni pizza falling from the sky.

Unfortunately for them it was nuclear-tipped.

A BIG WAD OF CASH

Charlie's mom was convinced werewolves were roaming the woods near her house. She asked Charlie to buy her a pistol and silver bullets for Mothers day. Charlie complied and spent $600 for a pistol and $5,732 for a box of 50 sterling silver bullets.

She loved his gift. "Those damn werewolves are gonna be sorry if they ever show up around here!" she exclaimed.

Next day, she was found dead. The pistol and empty bullet box were in her lap. Though she'd fired all 50, no other bodies were found. Cops were mystified.

Nobody knew the woods near her house were infested with zombies who sounded like werewolves when they howled. Also unknown was that those zombies also celebrated Mother's Day. One named Waldo decided to surprise his mom with a toaster for Mother's Day. Before leaving for Wal-Mart to steal one, because zombies don't have cash, checks, or credit cards, Waldo's mom said she wanted fresh human brains for Mother's Day. Waldo and two friends invaded Charlie's mom's house to get some.

Mom fought them valiantly. However, zombies can't be stopped by bullets - silver or otherwise.

After delivering fresh, steaming brains to his delighted mom, Waldo and his friends removed 50 silver slugs from their bodies, melted them, formed them into ingots, and sold them to a precious metals dealer for $4,500.

Now, cops are searching for zombies who are carrying a big wad of cash.

FOOD FADS

"Zombies are on the rampage!" Charlie yelled over his cell phone. "They'll probably reach your place by sundown."

"Thanks for letting me know," Bill said. "I'll leave town right now."

"No need to if you have Oreo cookies. Zombies prefer them to brains."

"I never heard anything so crazy."

"It's true," Charlie said. "I saw it on the Food Channel. They were talking about food fads of the undead, and how today's more sophisticated zombies have acquired tastes for stuff other than brains. The King of The Zombies explained it all. Then the host said, 'This is great news. Remember folks—if you're in the path of rampaging zombies, just offer then Oreos and they won't harm you."

"Thanks for telling me, Charlie. I'm glad I don't have to run for my life."

Later, when dozens of marauding zombies approached Bill's house, he rushed outside with a cookie jar crammed with Oreos.

"Hi guys. Have some Oreos."

Snickering, the zombies grabbed him and bit his skull open.

"Why?" Bill screamed.

"Oreos are out. Chocolate chip cookies are in. Got any?"

"No."

"Tough break," one of them said, as he pulled out a razor sharp ice cream scoop and went to work on Bills brains. "I guess he didn't see us on the Food Channel yesterday when we discussed our very latest food fads."

ZANKER'S SERUM

Dr. Zanker invented an amazing serum. When inoculated with his miracle drug, vampires stopped sucking blood from necks. The nation rejoiced!

However, there was an unanticipated side effect: vampires now craved peanut butter and sucked it from jars. Before long, they eliminated the nation's entire supply, including stocks earmarked for free distribution to senior citizens. This caused the great Peanut Butter Famine Riots of 2009 in which millions of disgruntled seniors, peanut butter lovers, and fans of blood-sucking vampire literature tore up the nation's cities.

Zanker was sued by movie and TV studios, the Amalgamated Brotherhood of Horror Writers, and the Association For The Advancement of Peanut Butter And Jelly Sandwich Eaters. Complaining bitterly to the Supreme Court, they proclaimed, "We want our beloved, blood-sucking vampires back. Who wants to read stories or see movies about hokey, peanut butter sucking vampires? Who wants to eat lousy-tasting, soy, peanut butter substitutes?"

Congress declared peanut butter an endangered species. The Court found Zanker guilty of destroying an entire literary genre and causing the near extinction of a beloved commodity. Declaring him Public Enemy Number One, they executed him on live TV. The nation rejoiced.

After a herculean effort rivaling the project to put a man on the Moon, an antidote was discovered. Soon, vampires once again preferred human blood to peanut butter. A National Holiday was declared. The nation rejoiced.

Note well, Do-Gooders: don't screw with the status quo like Zanker. Remember: no good deed ever goes unpunished.

AMNESIA

As a nurse pushed a gurney into the X-ray Room, the patient yelled, "Help! I can't remember my name!"

"Amazing, how so many arrive with amnesia," said the X-Ray doctor.

"Why do you suppose that is, Doctor?"

"Could be a structural weakness. When you have two heads, you have operational redundancy. So, if something happens to injure one head, the other takes over instantly. But, unlike us, this Earthling is cursed with a single head—a most ugly one. Seems when most Earthlings are transported from their planet, the trauma leads to amnesia. On the other hand, maybe they whacked his head during the abduction. That could've caused it, too."

"That box wasn't checked on the Abduction Form," she said.

"Maybe they forgot to check it. Wouldn't surprise me. The Ministry of Abductions hires lots of incompetents these days. Blame it on our manpower shortage from our war with Saturn. Seems like only the dregs are left." He asked the patient, "Did they strike your head with anything?"

"I can't remember. Who am I? Where am I?"

Ignoring his questions, the doctor told the nurse, "X-rays will tell all. I hope he only has amnesia. If he snaps out of it before he's roasted, he'll taste even better."

"Why is that?"

"Nobody knows for sure. But I hope we can cure his amnesia. He's got white hair. My children particularly enjoy the white-haired ones for dessert."

RETALIATION

Haitian zombies love chocolate chip cookies. When they discovered that Americans spend billions on Halloween treats, they assumed treats meant chocolate chip cookies. Consequently, 372,928 zombies hired Mexican Coyotes to smuggle them into America.

Homeland Security found out. The President canceled Halloween. Meanwhile, Congress rushed through a bill to provide chain saws to every American household.

Zombies don't watch TV or read newspapers, so they were unaware of this.

On Halloween night, all the zombies went trick-or-treating for chocolate chip cookies. All 372,928 were destroyed by chain saws when they rang doorbells.

Every scrap of putrid zombie remains was collected, ground, and packaged. Falsely labeled as "Prime Ground Beef," twenty million pounds were shipped to China.

One pound for every poisonous toy China has exported to America.

BACK HOME AFTER WAR'S END

America was heavily nuked during World War Seven.

When the war finally ended, the Army pulled us out of Oceana, and sent us home.

The first day back in America, Sarah and I strolled along desert sands at the edge of the ocean.

"Don't go too close to the water," she said. "It's still highly radioactive."

"It's the same way in Oceana," I said. "I can't get over how different everything looks around here. It's not the America I once knew."

"Yes. It's heartbreaking. Those nuclear missiles that hit us were terribly destructive."

"Still, it's wonderful to be back in Las Vegas watching the sunset over the Atlantic Ocean."

A VITAL QUESTION

"When will the world end?" I asked Swami Salami.

"In about 3 days."

"Can you be more precise?"

"No. Solar flares are interfering with the vibes I receive from The Illustrious Poobah."

"Can you call him?"

"That'd be outrageously expensive. He resides in another galaxy."

"The precise time of the end of the world is vital to my interplanetary business interests," I said. "Make the call and charge it to me."

"That's very good of you. Everyone in the universe will be indebted to you for your fabulous generosity."

Swami Salami made the call.

"The World will end in two days, twenty-one minutes, and thirty-seven seconds," said The Illustrious Poobah.

He lied!

Three weeks later, I've got a long distance phone bill for $740,387,821,492,184.

I'd appreciate if everyone who reads this sends a donation to help me. I just need $928,727 from every person in the universe.

Unfortunately, donations are not tax deductible.

A WONDERFUL BIRD

"I just landed on Mars," Jim told Houston Mission Control via wrist radio.

Sunspots blocked Houston's reply.

When Jim left his spaceship to plant a flag and claim Mars for his nation, Martians grabbed him. They took him to the Emperor's palace.

Scrutinizing Jim, the Emperor asked, "What is this strange looking creature?"

"We think it is a bird from another planet," said an advisor.

Jim figured he better hop around and whistle like a bird. His performance was so convincing, the Emperor applauded and said, "What a wonderful bird. I want him for a pet."

Jim was fed, bathed, groomed, and allowed to run loose through the Emperor's magnificent palace.

Days later, as he lollygagged in the Emperor's well-stocked harem, he radioed Houston. "Life's fantastic here. I'm treated like the Emperor's favorite pet. I'm giving you two week's notice that I'm resignation from the Space Agency. Tell my family that I'm never coming back."

Huston responded, "Martian's love (garbled) pets."

"Please repeat," Jim said. "Your message was garbled."

Sunspots blocked Huston's retransmissions.

When Martians tossed Jim onto blazing charcoals, he realized the missing words in Huston's message were: TO EAT.

MARTIAN BEAUTY STANDARDS

I saw an ad in the local paper: "Starving Martian Students Pet Beautifying Service will be in town for two weeks. For $1, we guarantee we'll groom your pet to the highest Martian beauty standards. Help us earn enough to pay our continuously escalating tuition costs. Call now for appointment!"

I figured things must be really tough if they had to come all the way to Earth to raise money. Since I'm all for higher education, I called and made an appointment.

When the Martian rang my doorbell, I gave him a dollar and my ugly old dog, Brutus. He put Brutus into a weird-looking machine the size of a Greyhound bus.

After a few minutes of grinding noise, out popped a block of ice. Brutus was inside.

"Doesn't he look wonderful?" asked the alien.

Brutus' head was on backwards. Two legs were missing.

"You killed my dog!" I screamed.

"No. He's still alive. He'll defrost in 12 hours."

"But he's uglier than before. Your ad said very clearly that you'd groom my pet to the highest Martian beauty standards.

"I did," said the student, as he drove off.

DIVINE MISSION

World War Seven broke out while I inspected the Doomsday Shelter seventeen miles below Area 51. Incommunicado, I didn't even know.

I was there only three days. But during that time, Martians waged nuclear war, won, and departed Earth with the spoils.

I checked nearby Las Vegas. No survivors. I checked other cities. Same thing. Horrors! Beside me, the only other survivors were cockroaches.

Fortunately, the Doomsday Shelter had lotsa supplies. Except for human companionship, life was normal.

Months passed. I was dying of loneliness. Then it dawned on me: I had a divine mission.

I contacted the King of the cockroaches. When I discussed my plan, he agreed.

We held a beauty contest. I married the winner.

We've mated hourly to repopulate Earth. It's working. When we have sufficient offspring, I'll build a humongous army, nuclear weapons, and rocket ships. Then we'll get revenge.

Beware, you genocidal Martian bastards! The cocka-humans are coming.

CHARLIE'S AMAZING BATHING SUIT

Charlie was certain he'd invented a shark-repellent bathing suit. After dipping his polka dot bathing suit in a mixture of chicken soup and dill pickle juice, he put it on, then jumped into the most dangerous shark-infested area of the Pacific.

Within minutes, ten great white sharks sensed his presence and raced toward him. The moment they spotted his bathing suit, they screamed and swam away at top speed. Later that day, the Coast Guard found their carcasses floating on the surface. Autopsies indicated the sharks had been scared to death.

CNN offered Charlie a million dollars to repeat the test on live television. The event was advertised around the clock for a week in advance.

On the appointed day, Charlie jumped into the ocean wearing his amazing bathing suit. Billions of TV watchers held their breath as underwater cameras showed dozens of great whites rushing toward Charlie. Everyone cheered when the sharks screamed, broke off their attack, and headed in the opposite direction.

The next day, CNN televised Charlie's funeral.

Nobody knew Loch Ness Monsters considered polka dot bathing suits dipped in chicken soup and dill pickle juice as gourmet treats, and that they'd swim thousands of miles just to eat one.

DISBELIEF

As Frank and Lisa came down the path in the most isolated section of the park, a man rose from a bench and disappeared in the surrounding bushes. The couple was so involved in discussing their failing finances, they didn't notice the shopping bag he left behind until they sat on the bench.

"Looks like somebody forgot their stuff," Frank said, pointing to the Barnes and Noble bag. He looked around, but didn't see anybody. Opening the bag, he found a leatherbound book. Attached to the cover was a bright yellow sticky-note.

"What does the note say?" Lisa asked.

"Do not open this book under any circumstances—unless you believe," Frank replied. "What the hell's that supposed to mean? Believe in what? I swear, the world gets weirder every day."

"Put it back and let's get outta here."

"Not until I open it."

"Are you crazy? What if it's cursed?"

"Geez, Lisa, stop being so superstitious. It's only a book."

Frank flipped through the pages. "Well if this ain't the damndest thing. Every page is blank."

"Let me see," Lisa said.

When he gave her the book, she screamed and dropped it.

"What happened?" he asked.

"It burned my hands!"

Frank checked her skin for redness. "I don't see a thing. You've been so jittery since you got laid off. I told you not to worry, we'll find a way to pay the mortgage. We'll start by having a garage sale. I'll bet I can get five bucks for this book."

He ignored Lisa's pleas about not bringing the spooky book back to their house.

That evening, Frank watched a World War Two espionage movie on TV. A secret agent was stopped at the French-German border by Guards who quizzed him about a blank notebook in his attaché case. He told interrogators he'd brought it to record travel expenses. Finding nothing incriminating, the guards waved him on. Once the agent was in a safe house, he coated the notebook's pages with chemicals. Words suddenly appeared that gave details on Nazi Germany's progress in developing the world's first nuclear bomb.

"Invisible ink!" Frank muttered. "Why didn't I think of that?"

Checking Google, he found information about invisible inks and how to make them visible. The easiest way was to pass the pages under black light.

Hurrying to Wal-Mart, he bought a black light. The moment he passed the first page of the book under the light, words appeared.

"Lisa! Look at this. You ain't gonna believe your eyes! President John F. Kennedy's name is printed on the first page.

"What does it say about him?" she asked.

"Nothing. Only his name appears. The rest is blank."

"Please get rid of that thing. It gives me the creeps."

Ignoring her, Frank turned to the next page. "This page has Amelia Earhart's name. I remember reading about her in school. She was a famous woman pilot who disappeared while flying across the Pacific in the 1930s."

The next page had Marilyn Monroe's name, but nothing else.

"This page has Elvis Presley's name," he said. "And this one has Jimmy Hoffa's. He was that union president who disappeared back in the '70s. They never found his body."

"Did you check the cover?" Lisa asked.

"No. Didn't think of it."

When Frank passed the cover under black light, large, hand printed letters appeared that said, "PEOPLE I'VE KILLED."

"What the hell's going on?" Lisa asked.

"I don't know."

"I'm calling the police. This might be the work of a serial killer." While she reached for the phone, he checked the back cover.

"Put the phone down," he said. "They'll never believe you."

"Why?"

"Because of what the back cover says. He read aloud, "I warned them not to stop believing. But they didn't listen. And to whoever finds this book and reads these names, I warn you, you better believe or your name will end up on these pages."

"Believe in what?" Lisa asked."

"The Boogie Man," Frank said. "He signed his name under the warning."

"That's the craziest thing I ever heard. The Boogie Man can't write. He's a monster, for goodness sakes. Geez, the way I'm talking, you'd think he actually exists."

"When did you find out he didn't?"

"I never believed in a stupid thing called the Boogie Man who lurked in the dark waiting to pounce on disobedient children," she said.

"I bought it all. The Easter Bunny, Tooth Fairy, Santa Claus, Boogie Man. I was devastated when I found out it was all just a big lie. Sometimes, for the fun of it, I wish I still believed."

Lisa called her husband a jerk.

That night, Frank and Lisa were murdered.

Homicide investigators still wonder about the leather-bound book they found near the victims' bodies and fingerprints on the book that the FBI, Scotland Yard, and Interpol couldn't identify.

Had detectives passed the book under black light, they would have noticed Frank and Lisa's names on the page following Jimmy Hoffa's, plus their murderer's name on the back cover.

BOREDOM

"Hey you, get out of the way!" a cop yelled. "Let the medics through."

Jason realized the cop was pointing a baton in his direction. He moved aside quickly when he saw paramedics carrying a stretcher. As they passed him, he almost threw up at the sight of the bloody, mangled mass that used to be a face.

"Looks like the Face Ripper struck again," said the stranger next to Jason. "Another beautiful woman bites the dust. If this keeps up, there won't be any good looking women left in this town."

"Geez. I didn't know you guys had a serial killer problem. Otherwise, I never woulda turned off the Interstate to grab a meal."

"Doesn't matter if you did. He only attacks females."

"How many did he kill so far?"

"Twenty-seven."

"What? How come I didn't hear about this on Fox News, or see it in the papers?"

"The politicians keep it quiet. Otherwise, nobody would come here. That'd put lotsa people outta work. The unemployment level is already bad enough in this burg."

Though the bloody sight should have killed his appetite, Jason found himself excited and hungrier.

"Is there a half-decent restaurant near here?" he asked.

"Minnie's Hash House is pretty good. It's just two blocks from here."

While eating meatloaf, Jason realized that the town might be the answer to his problems. Though he loved his stunning wife, Marcia, he was sick of her nagging. Plus, he was certain she was having a fling with a lawyer ten years his junior.

Returning home, he went to Wal-Mart and bought a dozen, hand-cranked LED lights. Then he drugged Marcia, put her and the lights in the car, and headed for the Face Ripper's town.

Arriving at the woods just outside town, he laid her on the ground, cranked the lights, placed them around her to illuminate her form, and headed back to his car. As he approached his Mustang, he heard footsteps crunching autumn leaves.

"Who's there?" he called.

"Police. What's going on here?"

"I was driving by and saw strange lights in the woods. See them over there? I went to take a look. There's a woman laying on the ground. I think she's dead. I was just going to jump in my car and drive to town to report it."

The cop pulled his pistol. "Put your hands over your head and walk slowly toward your car. Now, put your palms against the car and spread your legs real wide."

"But I didn't do anything wrong," Jason said.

"I'll be the judge of that," the cop said, slapping cuffs on Jason's wrists. "Now turn around."

The cop shined a high-powered flashlight in Jason's face. "Hmm. Anybody ever tell you you're good looking?"

The next day, word spread quickly through town. A man was found dead in the woods with his face ripped apart, though a nearby, beautiful, unconscious woman wasn't touched.

Nobody knew what to make of it.

They didn't realize until four more good-looking men were killed that the Face Ripper was bored and needed a change of pace.

THE AREA 51 OPTION

Three weeks after the Second Zombie War ended, the Alpha Party held their national convention in Las Vegas. They nominated Esther Church as their party's candidate for the November presidential election. Church was the most radical politician in the Amalgamated States of America.

During her acceptance speech, Church electrified the nation when she said, "On the first day that I'm the President of this great nation, I will issue an executive order to release all zombie prisoners of war and grant them full civil rights."

Five thousand party delegates cheered wildly for two minutes.

"It's time for change in Washington. It's time for love and compassion."

More cheers and applause.

"We all know there hasn't been an ounce of love or compassion in Washington since Harlan Kirk became President. The fact that we've had another zombie war in which forty thousand zombies were massacred and ten thousand were captured is stark proof. There's only one reason why this nation went to war: President Kirk and the Omega Party are warmongers. They started this war to fatten the wallets of bankers and the military-industrial complex."

The audience booed and raised their middle fingers.

"Yesterday, I called the President and asked him to reveal where he's hiding ten thousand zombie war prisoners. He hung up on me. Do you know why? Because he fears love and compassion. And he doesn't want you to know that the POWs are being brutally tortured."

More boos.

"Fortunately, we've been able to discover where they're imprisoned. In a salt mine. Without lights. Without food. Without water. Without sanitary facilities. And soon, they'll be executed without trials."

Sounds of anger and dismay filled the convention center.

"This is not the first time in the history of this country that zombie POWs have been horribly mistreated. A film recently discovered in government archives shows what this nation did fifty years ago to four thousand zombies captured during the First Zombie War. I have that film here today. Before I show it to you, I want you to remember what our history teachers taught us about the fate of those four thousand zombies. Does anybody remember where they were sent?"

"To a beautiful Pacific Island," shouted a delegate from Ohio.

"That's right. And we were also taught that they were allowed to live out their lives on that island. Further, we were told every attempt was made to transform them from brain eaters to vegetarians. Our history books said the transition was successful, and the zombies lived happily ever after. We were even quizzed on this episode of our nation's history. Well, guess what? Our teachers lied!"

Sounds of shock filled the convention center.

"So much for our pitiful educational system. But teachers weren't the only liars. Several weeks ago, the Historical Channel ran a program on TV about the last zombie prisoner held on that island. What her life had been like. And how she died in her sleep in that lush, island paradise. That too was a bunch of lies. So, if you're wondering what really happened to four thousand zombie POWs after the First Zombie War, here's the answer."

Several large screens descended from the ceiling. When the lights dimmed, delegates and millions of the nation's TV watchers gasped when they saw thousands of naked, emaciated zombie POWs jam-packed inside an open-air sports arena. Their decaying hands were raised overhead, as if begging for mercy. A silver-colored blimp approached the arena. When it was directly overhead, the crew opened portholes and dropped hundreds of baseball-sized napalm bombs onto the zombie hordes. Close ups of the crew showed them laughing, as they rained destruction into the arena.

Delegates shouted, "Killers! Murderers!" Many screamed at the sight of the zombies bursting into flames and tearing each other to pieces as they attempted to flee the holocaust.

When the five-minute film ended, Esther Church said, "Brothers and sisters of the Alpha Party, these horrible images will haunt my dreams for the rest of my life."

TV cameras panned the delegates. All looked shocked. Many were weeping.

"Unfortunately, I am the bearer of some very horrible news. As you know, our most recent zombie war ended just three weeks ago. Since then, ten thousand zombie prisoners have been held in very desperate circumstances in a salt mine. Brace yourselves for what I'm about to tell you. President Kirk plans to execute them the same way you just saw in the film. By napalm bombs dropped from a blimp."

Raising a clenched fist, she shouted, "We must never allow zombie genocide to happen in this nation again!"

The audience screamed, "Never again...never again...never again."

Someone ran onto the stage with an effigy of President Kirk. When Church set it on fire, the roaring crowd could be heard a mile away.

* * * *

Harlan Kirk and members of his Cabinet were watching the proceedings in a White House conference room.

"She's a rotten, lying, psycho bastard," said the Attorney General. "That film's a total fabrication. Nothing like that ever happened."

"But you have to admit," said Kirk, "it's an extremely effective piece of propaganda. Did you see how those nuts in the convention center were crying and pulling their hair out over lies? Why aren't our public relations people dreaming up dynamite stuff like that?"

The Secretary of Defense said, "I never thought I'd see the day when Americans would carry on over a bunch of bloodthirsty, brain-eating zombies. To show what a liar she is, I think we should release the film that shows what really happened to the POWs after the First Zombie War."

"If we do that, we may cause an even bigger uproar," said the President. "If that crowd went insane over a lie about napalming prisoners, imagine how they'll react to the truth about them being nuked on a Pacific atoll, fifty years ago. Hell, the minute they find out we plan to do the same to our POWs, the opposition will tear this country apart. We better destroy those damn zombies some other way. Any ideas?"

"Why not napalm them like we saw in Church's phony film?" asked the Secretary of the Air Force. "We have a plenty of napalm bombs."

"If we do that," said the Secretary of the Army, "we'd give credence to Esther Church's ridiculous lies. Need I remind everyone that the press, which is so hostile to this administration, would immediately broadcast the time and place of the executions. The opposition party would bus in rent-a-mobs to surround the stadium. They might even try to shoot down the blimp. Things could get worse if our supporters showed up. Both sides might start shooting at each other. The last thing we need is Americans killing Americans over brain-eating zombies."

"So, what do you suggest as an alternative?" asked the President.

"Since the POWs are being held in a salt mine, let's pump in napalm and fry the bastards."

"How soon can that be done?"

"In a matter of hours."

"Good. Let's do it tonight at midnight. The sooner those damn POWs are out of the way, the sooner I can begin concentrating on my reelection. Now let's watch more of that blasted convention to see what else that idiot has on her twisted, bird brain."

"This nation's fed up with Harlan Kirk and the Omega Party," Church said to her spellbound audience. "Where has their warmongering policies gotten us?"

"Nowhere," delegates shouted.

"If things don't change drastically in Washington, we face the real possibility of a third zombie war. We cannot let that happen. It's time for change. Time for new ideas. Time for new leadership. Time to give zombies love, compassion, and a piece of the American pie."

The audience yelled, whistled, applauded.

"And now, as your nominee for the highest office in this nation, I want to offer you a new symbol for our party. Though a dove has served us well for so many years, it no longer represents the invigorated spirit and aspirations of this magnificent party."

As a band played a fanfare, Esther pulled a golden cord. A red, white and blue curtain fell revealing a huge painting. Sounds of appreciation filled the auditorium at the sight of a little blonde girl facing a tall, smiling zombie. Both wore white, flowing robes reminiscent of ancient Greece. In the girl's hand was a cuddly, stuffed koala bear, which she extended toward the zombie.

Hundreds of ushers quickly passed out stuffed koalas to every delegate, as a particularly moving arrangement of *Love Is Everything This Cruel World Will Ever Need* filled the auditorium.

Hugging their koalas, teary-eyed delegates sang the party's official song.

President Kirk cursed aloud. "Zombies in flowing robes. Good grief. What next? Don't they know that anybody who tries to hand a zombie a stuffed animal will get his fool head torn off? Esther Church is not only a damn idiot, she's the most dangerous woman in this nation. She must be stopped."

"Consider it done," said the Director of GIA, the Global Intelligence Agency. "With your permission, I'll implement the Area 51 Option."

"Terrific idea. Yes, by all means do it. Oh, this is going to be rich." Raising his glass of fine bourbon, the President added. "Let's toast the geniuses of the GIA who created the Area 51 Option."

After they drank, the Secretary of the Treasury asked, "What's the Area 51 Option?"

"The ace up our sleeve," said the President, chuckling.

At midnight, the Army secretly napalmed all ten thousand zombie POWs, as they loitered in a salt mine deep below the Nevada desert.

The next day, Kirk held a press conference. "I'd like to make an announcement, then I'll take some questions. In the spirit of bipartisan cooperation, I've offered Esther Church, the Alpha Party's presidential nominee, an opportunity to personally meet with zombie POWs so she can explain her aspirations to them. She has accepted. A plane will be provided so she and members of the press can fly to the site where the POWs are being scrupulously cared for. The reporters who accompany her will also be granted time to interview the prisoners. I'm pleased to tell you that she has agreed. She'll visit them tomorrow."

The journalists applauded.

"As to the zombie POWs, we intend to handle them humanely, just like President Holmes did at the end of the First Zombie War. They'll be transported to a Pacific island where scientists will transform them from brain eaters to vegetarians. Isolated from the rest of the world, they'll be allowed to live out their lives in peace and dignity.

I know some in the Alpha Party have claimed that zombie POWs were never treated humanely, and that our history books and teachers have lied. That's not true. Frankly, I'm concerned over the politicization of the zombie wars and POWs by the opposition. I think they owe an apology to every teacher in this nation for calling them liars. I call upon the leadership of the Alpha Party to do so as quickly as possible to ensure our citizens retain faith in our educational institutions.

Meanwhile, we are still trying to determine which nation recruited, trained, equipped, and transported the zombies who attacked our nation last Christmas. Rest assured, we will find out. And we will take appropriate action against the nation or nations that perpetrated this unprovoked sneak attack on the Amalgamated States of America. And now, I'll take some questions."

"I'm Harry Smith of *World International* Press. Esther Church says the zombie freedom fighters are being held as political prisoners in a salt mine under primitive and inhumane conditions. If that's true, this nation has violated every treaty we've signed regarding the disposition of captured combatants."

"First of all, I don't know why you called them freedom fighters. They're vicious renegades who would've torn off the heads and eaten the brains of every man, woman, and child in America, if our magnificent troops hadn't stopped them. Secondly, Esther Church is dead wrong about the conditions under which zombies are being held. They are being kept in very pleasant surroundings above ground where every facility is available to them. I assure you that the Omega Party has just as much concern about the welfare of zombie prisoners as the Alpha Party."

"Exactly where are they being held?" asked a female journalist from the *Philadelphia Times*.

"For security reasons, I don't think it's wise to identify the location at this time. Especially since Esther Church will be going there tomorrow. My concerns are that some rogue zombies might have evaded capture, and might still be hiding. In fact they may be listening to this press conference at this very moment. And if any are, I strongly urge all zombies who have not yet surrendered to do so as quickly as possible. They can turn themselves into any military facility, fire station, or police station in the nation. They have my personal guarantee that they'll be treated fairly."

"I'm Sally Saunders of the *London Afternoon Daily*. I've heard a rumor that the zombie POWs have already been executed."

"Well, you can ask Esther Church about that after she visits all ten thousand of them tomorrow."

While a few in the press corps chuckled, President Kirk tried to visualize what it might have looked like inside the mine hours earlier when all the POWs they were now discussing were destroyed by napalm.

"Mr. President," said another reporter. "When the war ended last month, you claimed the zombies were a new type that had never been seen before, and that they were parachuted into Arizona on Christmas Day from unmarked, stealth aircraft. You said only a demon nation would so such a thing. On the other hand, Esther Church said nothing like that every happened. She claims this new type of zombie has actually been residing in Arizona for several years, and that they arrived on foot by crossing the border from Mexico. And because of that, they should be considered undocumented aliens, not hostile zombie invaders. Since nobody has found any parachutes, or ever reported seeing any aircraft dropping zombies, will you admit that she's right about where the zombies came from, and that they should be treated like undocumented aliens instead of POWs?"

"She's dead wrong on all counts. Approximately fifty thousand zombies parachuted into this nation on Christmas Day. None of the stealth aircraft transporting them was detected by our defense systems. Our Global Intelligence Agency is still investigating to determine where they came from. And while we're on the subject, the demon nation that did this to the American people will pay a terrible price."

"I have a follow-up question, Sir. Lets say it happened the way you've described. And the GIA determines that the so-called demon nation was Switzerland. Exactly what would you do to Switzerland?"

"That beautiful, mountainous country would be transformed into a bleak, flat-as-a-pancake desert situated several hundred feet below sea level."

"Thank you, Mr. President," said Kirk's Chief of Staff to signal the end of the press conference.

The next day, Esther Church and six reporters, who championed her causes, were picked up at their Las Vegas hotels by a limo secretly owned by the GIA. When they entered the limo, the driver, who was separated from them by a glass panel, pressed a button that released exotic gases into the passenger compartment. In twenty-three seconds, Church and her entourage were in a pleasant stupor. Independent thinking became impossible and would remain so for at least ten hours.

This was the most dangerous part of the GIA's top secret scenario. If random, unprocessed, contaminated information were inadvertently introduced from outside the limo, Esther and the reporters could react by committing murder and unspeakable atrocities upon each other.

An Army liaison officer sitting next to the driver pointed a satellite-monitored laser pen at Esther's forehead. A soft beep verified her brain's readiness for satellite input. He did the same to the other passengers.

In the deluded minds of Esther and the reporters, they thought there were driven to the Las Vegas airport where they boarded a plush government jet for a two-hour flight. But they never left the limo.

Later on, they'd remark among themselves about the delicious hors d'oueuvres they were served on the jet, as it headed to Camp Pleasant. None of them would ever learn that Camp Pleasant was a nonexistent location. Nor would they discover they had never left the limo. The two-hour flight they experienced in their chemically induced delusional state was, in reality, a twenty minute limo ride from downtown Las Vegas to a vacant warehouse on the outskirts of Vegas.

When the limo reached North Las Vegas, it entered a vacant warehouse owned by the GIA.

"Welcome to Camp Pleasant," said the GIA agent who opened the limo doors. "I hope you had a pleasant flight."

"It was very nice," Esther said, "except for some turbulence over New Mexico."

Viewing what appeared to her as wonderfully manicured, tropical surroundings, she added, "How gorgeous. I had no idea the Army has such a delightful military base. If I didn't know better, I'd swear I was in Beverly Hills."

As her words echoed throughout the empty warehouse, she made a mental note to make Camp Pleasant her Presidential Retreat after she was elected President.

"America has always honored and cared for its enemy prisoners in special ways," the agent said, "especially when they're zombies. Would you like a snack before meeting them?"

"That'd be nice."

"Let's go to the gazebo, which is just to the left of the rose garden. The zombies have prepared some treats for you."

Though they stood in the same place in the warehouse the whole time, the visitors saw themselves walking toward a nonexistent gazebo. Several remarked about the beauty of the roses on both sides of the immaculate walkway.

"Yes, they are quite remarkable," said the agent. "Several zombie volunteers maintain the gardens."

The visitors saw two zombies in tailored, sky blue jump suits waving from the other end of the rose garden where they were weeding. Both were guarded by American soldiers who carried flamethrowers.

Inside the gazebo was a table loaded with treats fit for a king.

"Oh, what are those big, luscious looking powdered things?" a female reporter asked.

"Jelly donuts," said the agent. "They're baked right here by our prisoners."

"I never saw jelly donuts the size of cantaloupes."

"Well, zombies will be zombies," he chuckled. "They tend to exaggerate everything. To expand their very limited outlook on life, we encourage them to be creative. By the way, they baked these especially for you. Try some. You'll find them quite delicious. So are the éclairs they made."

The visitors couldn't get over how wonderful everything tasted.

After a leisurely repast of things imagined, Church said, "May we please interview the zombies now?"

"Certainly. They're eagerly awaiting your arrival."

One of the male reporters grabbed a donut to carry along. He screamed horribly when it transformed into his four-year old daughter's bloody, severed head.

"Dammit," the agent yelled to a panel of GIA doctors who were monitoring the proceedings. "You assured me there'd be no anomalies in the Delusional Scenario."

"Sorry about that," a doctor said, as she sprayed a fine mist into the reporter's eyes. "It's one of those gremlins that show up from time to time. Could be a solar flare interfering with satellite transmissions. No way around it. He's okay now. This'll erase whatever he just saw from his memory."

"What do you think he saw?"

"Oh, there are dozens of possibilities. None are pleasant."

"You sure he won't remember the unpleasant image, but will remember everything else in the Delusion Scenario?"

"Positive."

The visitors engaged in pleasant chatter as they approached a large field where they saw ten thousand zombies in blue jump suits sitting quietly in padded folding chairs. The field was surrounded by hundreds of soldiers armed with flamethrowers and chainsaws.

As the visitors approached, the zombies stood up and applauded.

Esther mounted a stage equipped with a lectern and several microphones. In reality, she hadn't moved from the place in the warehouse she'd occupied since leaving the limo.

"Ladies and gentlemen of the zombie community, I greet you as a friend," Church said.

The zombies applauded again.

"You are the ugliest bunch of bastards, I've ever seen!" she yelled. "I'm getting the hell out of here!"

A doctor quickly sprayed mist into Church's eyes. Others made notations on their clipboards. Another medic pointed a laser pen at her forehead. The pen beeped softly when it received feedback from an orbiting GIA satellite. Within seconds, appropriate sections of her memory banks were erased.

"That's the second anomaly in the Delusional Scenario," said the agent. I hope there aren't any more."

"The fact is," said a doctor, "we usually need at least three months to program a scenario. The White House only gave us twelve hours for this project. I'm amazed worse things haven't happened."

Church spoke again to the assembled zombies that existed only in her deluded mind. "I'm Esther Church. I was nominated by the Alpha Party to run for President of the Amalgamated States. I expect to win the election in November. When I do, I promise to do two things for you. First I'll grant you amnesty. Second, I'll grant you full civil rights. That means you'll become automatic American citizens."

A one-armed zombie raised his hand.

When Church acknowledged him, he asked, "What's amnesty."

She spent several minutes explaining.

Another hand went up.

"What's civil rights?" asked a female zombie whose head was half missing.

This lead to an exchange between the zombies and Church about the Alpha Party's ideology, peppered with heavy doses of her radical social ideas.

Meanwhile, the reporters took down every word.

Twenty minutes later, Church said, "Thank you for your kind attention. And now members of the press will interview you."

"What's the press?" asked a zombie.

"I'll let Harry Zimmer from the *New York Daily Bugle* explain it to you. He's the dean of the White House Press Corps."

"What's the White House?" a zombie asked.

"What's up with these dumb questions?" the GIA agent asked doctors, as he read the script of what was occurring only within the minds of the visitors.

"Some of our whiz kids decided to inject a bit of humor," a doctor said. "It sounds ludicrous to us as we read the paper script, but it sounds perfectly normal in the minds of our visitors and what they are experiencing."

"Damn jerks!" the agent said. "Make sure you mention all this clowning around with the script during the post mortem meeting when we get back to Area 51. If you don't, I will."

When Church finished her discussion, she gave the floor to the reporters. They interviewed the zombies and thanked them for being so candid.

A woman's voice rang out from the audience. "Hi, Esther."

"Geez," Church said, "that sounds like my mom."

"It is your mom," said the voice. "I'm in the second row, sitting on the lap of this nice zombie."

"What are you doing here, Mom?"

"Just visiting some of the folks you've promised to make citizens. I sure hope this nice zombie man moves next door to me."

Suddenly, the zombie tore Mom's head off. Holding her head by the ears, he placed the severed neck over his lips and drank the blood. Then he jammed his hand inside the neck, as if it were the opening of a cookie jar, tore out every bit of tissue within the skull, and ate it. Muscle, veins, brains, everything.

"Hey, don't be a hog," yelled the zombie next to him. "Pass her head around so we all can have some of those goodies."

"Help! Church screamed. "Somebody do something!"

The solders guarding the zombies didn't move.

"You cowardly bastards! As my party's nominee for President, I'm ordering you to attack. If you don't, I'll have you jailed."

The soldiers opened up with flamethrowers. The stench of burning zombie flesh filled the air.

The visitors saw themselves rushing back to the limo. Though the actual trip from the warehouse to the hotels on the Las Vegas Strip took only twenty-five minutes, in their heads they experienced a two-hour return airplane flight.

Church's script varied slightly from those of the reporters. Hers called for her to go unconscious from the moment the flamethrowers started, until she woke up in bed in her hotel room.

When she woke, the exotic sprays and gasses had worn off, and she was back to normal. But she was far from what psychiatrists would call normal. Every time she shut her eyes, the scene of her mother's decapitation ran through her head. No matter what she tried, she couldn't shake the horrible images. The Delusional Scenario had been so deeply embedded in her brain, the images would never leave her.

Terribly distressed, she called the hotel operator. A doctor was dispatched to her room. But, before he arrived, an overwhelming impulse—one of many embedded into her psyche by the scenario—drove her to the hotel window. Her body fell fifteen stories and slammed onto the roof of a passing cab.

The world's major newspapers carried the story. The banner headlines of the *New York Daily Mail* screamed, "TEN THOUSAND ZOMBIE POWS MASSACRED. CHURCH ORDERS THEIR DESTRUCTION, THEN COMMITS SUICIDE."

The memories that had been implanted in the visiting reporters' brains were identical. However, their script diverged from Church's, starting at the point where her mother appeared. They never saw or heard her mother. Instead, they saw Esther Church ask a zombie a question. When he didn't answer, she left the stage, slapped his face, and called him a dumb-ass zombie who deserved to die.

The zombie responded by spitting on her. Enraged, she demanded the soldiers do something to teach the zombie some manners. When the soldiers didn't act, she called them cowardly bastards. She grabbed one of the soldier's portable flamethrowers, pointed it at the nearest zombies, and torched them.

All hell broke loose. Zombies rushed her, forcing the soldiers to blast them with their flamethrowers. By the time it was over, all ten thousand had been destroyed. Esther Church was heard cackling and saying, "That'll fix the ugly bastards."

Before long, billions around the world, who heard the news, branded the late Esther Church as just another lying, hypocritical, petty politician who got what she deserved.

When Harlan Kirk and his Cabinet met, the President said to the Secretary of the Treasury, "That was the Area 51 Option. Wasn't it fantastic?"

* * * *

No one outside of the Global Intelligence Agency, including President Kirk and his Cabinet, knew about the ultra-secret Area 52 Option. The option that would be exercised soon after GIA whiz kids debugged the final version of the scenario. The option that would make the entire nation see that which wasn't there.

End

About the Author

Michael A. Kechula is a retired technical writer. His fiction has won first place in 9 contests and placed in 7 others. He's also won Editor's Choice awards 4 times. His stories have been published by 118 magazines and 32 anthologies in Australia, Canada, England, India, Scotland, and US. He's authored two books of flash and micro-fiction stories: "A Full Deck of Zombies--61 Speculative Fiction Tales" and "The Area 51 Option and 70 More Speculative Fiction Tales."

www.ingramcontent.com/pod-product-compliance
Lightning Source LLC
LaVergne TN
LVHW050638100826
845148LV00011B/1902

* 9 7 8 1 6 0 2 1 5 1 0 7 9 *